FITZ

A NOVEL

by
Mick Cochrane

Alfred A. Knopf ⋌ New York

THIS IS A BORZOI BOOK PUBLISHED BY ALFRED A. KNOPF

Visit us on the Web! randomhouse.com/teens

Educators and librarians, for a variety of teaching tools, visit us at
RHTeachersLibrarians.com

Library of Congress Cataloging-in-Publication Data
Cochrane, Mick.
Fitz : a novel / by Mick Cochrane. — 1st ed.
p.   cm.
"A Borzoi Book."
Summary: Fifteen-year-old Fitz kidnaps the father he has never known,
taking him from his St. Paul apartment building at gunpoint, in an attempt
to address his bewildering mix of resentment and yearning.
ISBN 978-0-375-85683-9 (trade) — ISBN 978-0-375-95683-6 (lib. bdg.) —
ISBN 978-0-375-89773-3 (ebook) — ISBN 978-0-375-84611-3 (pbk.)
[1. Fathers and sons—Fiction. 2. Kidnapping—Fiction. 3. Single-parent
families—Fiction. 4. Saint Paul (Minn.)—Fiction.] I. Title.
PZ7.C63972Fit 2012
[Fic]—dc23
2011042366

The text of this book is set in 11-point Goudy.

Printed in the United States of America

November 2012

10 9 8 7 6 5 4 3 2 1

First Edition

For Ron and Marlys Ousky

PROLOGUE

When Fitz was a little boy, he liked to imagine that his father was quietly, secretly watching over him, loving him, for his own good and unselfish reasons, from a distance. He imagined his father parking his car on their street late at night and looking up at his son's bedroom window. Thinking of the posters on the wall, the stuffed animals, the night-light. Longing to tuck him in, bring him a glass of water, tell him a story. Instead, making a wish, saying a simple prayer. This fantasy was so strong, so real in all its particulars, he imagined it so often, in such detail, Fitz sometimes found himself staring down from his bedroom window onto the street below, looking for his father's car.

NOT THE USUAL ANGST

On a cool morning in late May, Fitz is standing in the alley behind his father's apartment in St. Paul. Truth be told, lurking is what he's doing. Trying to act as if he belongs here, as if maybe he's waiting for a ride. Keeping an eye on the door, checking the clock on his phone from time to time, doing his best not to look suspicious, doing his best not to look criminal.

This is one of the fancier neighborhoods in the city—"the Historic Summit Hill District." That's what real-estate agents call it. It's where F. Scott Fitzgerald, the famous writer his mother named him for, lived a hundred years ago. It's full of yuppies—Geoffries and Jennas, his friend Caleb calls them, Pasta-Hounds. It's less than five miles away from where Fitz lives with his mother on the city's west side, but it took him forty minutes to get here on the bus. He had to cross one of the longest rivers in the world—the Mississippi—and transfer downtown.

His father's building is red stone, the walls thick as a castle's. It reminds Fitz of Fort Snelling, the frontier fort overlooking the river he's visited on school field trips. It's got turrets and pillars and balconies. A sleeping porch in the back. It must have been built at the turn of the last century, a mansion for some railroad or grain baron. Now it's divided into separate units: his father's, he's learned, is on the second floor.

Fitz has been in the entry—studied the names on the mailboxes, checked out the catalogs and magazines in the bin—but never beyond the heavy security door. He's never been in his father's apartment. He imagines hardwood floors, a fireplace, some kind of gourmet kitchen, a wine rack, a killer home-theater system. His father likes nice things, Fitz knows that much about him. His father's car—a shiny silver sedan, leather interior, five-speed stick—is parked in its assigned spot, twenty feet away from where Fitz is standing.

There's no litter in the alley, no broken glass. It's newly paved. Here they probably don't even call it an alley. That would be too common. There's some upscale equivalent—"anterior access road," that's what they call it, Fitz thinks, something like that.

A black SUV passes slowly. There's a woman inside, nicely dressed, wearing sunglasses, fluffing her hair in the rearview mirror. Fitz smiles pleasantly at her, trying his best not to look like a kidnapper, and she smiles back. To her, he probably looks like a typical fifteen-year-old boy. He's wearing sneakers, black jeans, a gray hoodie. He's got a backpack slung over his shoulder.

And that's exactly what he is: a typical fifteen-year-old boy. A sophomore on the B honor roll. A kid with a messy room, an electric guitar, a notebook full of song lyrics, vague dreams about doing something great someday, a crush on a red-haired girl. The city is full of kids like him. America is full of kids like him. He's nothing special.

Except that he's carrying a Smith & Wesson .38 revolver in the waistband of his jeans and a gutful of confusion, a lifetime's resentment in his heart. A gnawing hunger for a father he's never known.

He kneels down now, retying his shoes for the third or fourth time. Fitz can imagine his father inside, straightening his silk tie, sipping a cup of fresh-ground, free-trade coffee, thinking about his day—a meeting with a client maybe, a deposition—no idea that someone is waiting for him, that his son has other plans.

2

For more than a month now, ever since he discovered his father's home address, Fitz has been secretly observing him, tracking his movements. Not quite stalking, he tells himself, more like a cop on a stakeout. Fitz has discovered that he has a talent for invisibility. He's good at blending in. The week before, he was sitting in the lobby of the downtown building where his father's law firm has its offices. He was slouched in a chair, headphones on, reading, when his father got off the elevator and walked right by him. Fitz could have stuck his foot out and tripped him. He got up then and stood in line behind his father as he paid for his bottle of water and copy of the *New York Times* in the lobby snack bar, tailed him as he walked the half block to the ramp where he parked his car.

It started out as a kind of game. It was exciting. Every time he set out, there was some suspense. It was like going fishing. That same sense of anticipation. In this, Fitz, who can be easily bored and distracted, has patience. He's willing to wait. After nearly an hour of hanging out here last Saturday afternoon—his mom thought he was at band practice—Fitz saw his father emerge in shorts and a ball cap, and followed him to the local co-op. Watched him fill a basket with organic produce.

Fitz noticed things about his dad, and later, back home in his bedroom, he wrote them down in the notebook where he kept his songs. *Long fingers. Likes Granny Smith apples, red grapes. Doesn't check prices. Wallet full of twenties.* It felt top-secret and incriminating, like some kind of CIA dossier.

Gradually, after three or four of these outings, it became something more than a game for Fitz. Once, when he realized he'd missed his dad's departure from work, he felt such an unexpected crushing sadness. He'd had no idea how much it meant to him, how much was at stake.

He wrote a song about his dad, his building actually. He'd been thinking about the rough touch of those walls, their imposing, impenetrable mass. The U.S. Army built Fort Snelling because it was afraid of Indian raids. Fitz wondered what his father was afraid of.

You're living in a fortress,
You're living all alone.
You're living in a fortress
Trapped behind your walls of stone.

There's bars on your windows,
Double chain across your door.
There's bars on your windows,
So scared you don't go out no more.

Robbers and muggers and thieves,
The bad guys that you fear.
Robbers and muggers and thieves,
Watch out: they're drawing near.

When Fitz showed it to Caleb, he seemed impressed, as impressed as he ever got. "Not the usual angst," he said. Caleb played it as a slow blues in A, and Fitz followed along with a little walk on the bass. Caleb read Fitz's words off his crumpled notebook and sang them in his bluesman's growl, part Howlin' Wolf, part Cookie Monster. Caleb once confessed that he sometimes wished he were black, blind, born in the Delta. He is, in fact, white, sighted, and was born in South St. Paul. But Caleb has soul. His voice can sound ancient, ravaged and sinister, like something from a scratchy 78. He sang Fitz's song with great feeling, eyes closed. Hearing his words sung with such passion, thinking about his father's building, where he'd stood just the day before touching the rough stubble of the walls, Fitz felt something complicated and jagged working through his insides—not the usual angst, Caleb was right about that, it was something else entirely.

Before long, the crazy cat-and-mouse game with his father became more important to Fitz than his so-called real life. He still went to school, of course, he studied geometry and biology, he ate dinner with his mother and helped load the dishwasher. They talked about their days. He listened to music in his room and texted his friends. He played his bass. He stared at a yearbook picture of the lovely Nora Flynn and tried to think of an excuse to call her. But somehow, that life, that public routine, came to seem like just filling time, going through the motions.

It was a performance. That's what it was. A one-man show staged for the benefit of his mother, his teachers, his friends. He knew the script and he could pull it off. But Fitz the son, Fitz the student, Fitz the friend—that wasn't *him*. It was like him, it was a part of him. It's just that there was more to him than anyone realized.

He'd be working on a math problem, trying to figure out the area of some polygon, or he'd be talking to Caleb about some new song the two of them should try to work up, but all the while he'd be thinking about his father, planning his next spy mission. The real drama of his life had become secret, had gone underground.

At some point, watching was not enough. He was no longer satisfied being a spectator. He wanted to get off the sidelines, to get in the game. If seeing his father was a drug—sometimes it felt like that, mood-altering—he needed a stronger dose. Like the man in the Edgar Allan Poe story obsessed with the old guy's vulture eye, after a long period of secret watching, he felt compelled to action. That feeling in his gut when he saw his dad—he needed to do something about it.

This was his logic. He wanted to spend some time with his father, what was the phrase? *Quality time*. He wanted to spend some quality time with his dad. It was time to get acquainted. But his dad wasn't interested. After all these years, that much was obvious. It wasn't like he was going to respond to an invitation. Fitz figured he needed a convincer.

3

Fitz touches the gun he's got jammed in his jeans. It feels solid and reassuring. It has weight. It makes Fitz feel substantial. "This is a serious piece," that's what the kid who sold it to him said. They were standing on a playground after dark, underneath monkey bars Fitz used to climb. Fitz has known this kid for years—Dominic Rizzo. He calls himself the Dominator, but there really isn't anything dominant about him. Nobody much likes him. In elementary school, he stole things from other people's desks, worthless things—a dirty eraser, the stub of a pencil. He has a pinched, ratlike face and smells like an ashtray. He's been to juvie more than once.

But if you want to buy something—pills, weed, an ID, you name it—Dominic is your man. The playground is like his office. He sits on the tire swing, wobbling slowly back and forth, a cigarette cupped in his hand. When Fitz came by one night and told him he wanted to get a gun, he didn't seem all that surprised. He didn't ask questions. "I'm not going to shoot anybody," Fitz said, and tried to laugh. "I just want to make a point."

Dominic didn't seem to care. "Whatever," he said. "You want a dummy?" he asked. "A piece of crap? Or a serious piece?" Fitz told him he wanted the real thing. "Okay," Dominic told him. "Two hundred bucks. Be here Sunday night."

Fitz had a wad of money stashed in his desk. He'd been saving for a new bass—the thing he played was some rebuilt, no-name Frankenstein he'd found at a flea market. Sunday night Fitz told his mom he was going for a walk and brought his money to the playground. Dom took him into the park and retrieved a bag from behind some bushes. "Here she be," he said. "Thirty-eight snub-nose, the Chief's Special."

Dom showed him how to push the latch release forward and open the cylinder. He gave it a spin. He explained that the gun held five rounds and that he was giving him that many. "There's no safety," Dom said. Fitz knew what that meant, but somehow that phrase, those words—they made it seem as if Dom were telling him something bigger, more ominous.

"You're packing now," he told Fitz. "You got some serious street cred." Dom was making fun of him, Fitz was pretty sure, a law-abiding kid like him buying a gun, but he didn't really care. He needed to get his father's attention, and this would do the trick.

Now, with his hand on the gun, he feels like a serious person. Someone to be reckoned with. There have been times in the past couple of weeks when watching his father made Fitz feel small and insubstantial, unimportant. The feeling of excitement and purpose slipped away at those times, and he felt just like a nothing, a nobody. Easy to ignore, easy to blow off. Fitz is preoccupied with this man, who clearly gives him no more thought than he does the cable or electric bill or any other monthly obligation. Fitz is a witness to a rich and fascinating life that doesn't include him. He is on the outside looking in, his nose pressed against the glass.

Fitz understands that puny boys love their violent video games so much because playing them makes them feel big, powerful, dangerous. That has never been his thing. But now he has to admit it—his piece, this steel he's carrying, it makes him feel confident. Today his father is not going to blow him off. Today Fitz is going to make himself visible to his father.

4

The door to the building opens and a man steps out. Curtis Powell, Esquire. Partner in the firm of Plunkett and Daugherty. JD, cum laude, St. Paul College of Law, whose practice involves a balance of employment and complex commercial litigation, recipient of the Advocates for Human Rights Award. His father.

Fitz has memorized the biography and studied the picture of him on his law firm's website, a formal studio shot, like a school portrait—the same sort of vague blue background. To Fitz, the man in that picture looks pretty smart. He also looks pretty pleased with himself. He's pretty much right where he wants to be in life. He doesn't look at all like the kind of man who fathers a child and then has nothing to do with him for fifteen years other than scratching out a monthly check. But who does? Who looks like that guy?

This morning, in person, he looks only slightly less composed. He comes down the steps squinting into the morning sunlight. Like Fitz, his father is long-limbed and tall—he's a shade over six feet. Fitz is five-ten and still growing. He wears size eleven shoes, and his mom says he's going to grow into his feet like a big-pawed puppy. His father has more meat on him. His upper body looks thick, like he may have done some work with weights, but still he looks light on his feet, quick, graceful even, a tennis player—Fitz has seen a racket in his backseat. He's wearing a white shirt and dark suit, one of the bright ties he favors—this one is orange. His shoes are black, polished to an impossible sheen. He's got a black leather briefcase in one hand and his suit jacket slung over his shoulder on a hanger.

Fitz flips up his hood and takes a deep breath. He takes hold of the handle of the gun.

The thought crosses his mind: This is crazy. What am I doing? Kidnapping my own father. He feels himself starting to perspire. Fitz knows he's probably going to regret it. He's not stupid. There are going to be consequences. His life is never going to be the same, he feels that, he's going to put himself in a world of trouble. He doesn't have to go through with this. He could turn back now, catch a bus, head home, drop the gun in a sewer, crawl back into bed.

His father holds up his key ring and extends his arm toward his car, pointing, an unmistakable look of pleasure on his face—this is mine, his expression says, all this finely tuned German machinery. My beautiful car, my beautiful life. There's something about that expression that sets Fitz's feet in motion.

Fitz steps out into the alley. The lights of his father's car flash, and the locks pop up. His father hangs his suit jacket in the back, takes a minute to smooth it, adjusting it so that it drapes without

14

wrinkling, sets his bag on the backseat. His father still hasn't seen him. He's completely absorbed by what he's doing.

Fitz has witnessed this little ritual before: his father performs it every morning as he leaves for work and every evening as he prepares to come home. But there's something about it this time that enrages Fitz. This perfectly starched, self-satisfied man all alone in his well-tuned, tailored, wrinkle-free world—the sight of it makes Fitz wants to smash something.

His father closes the back door and is now getting himself settled behind the wheel. Fitz crosses the alley in a few quick strides, comes up on the car's passenger side, and pulls the door open. He leans down and peers inside the car. His father has been fiddling with the radio and looks up now, startled. Fitz has his hand on the gun, but it's still hidden under his sweatshirt.

"What?" his father says. "What do you need?" Maybe he thinks Fitz wants directions, maybe a handout—spare change for bus fare. Maybe he thinks he has a sad story to tell him. That's when Fitz takes the gun out. He doesn't so much point it as show it. It's a visual aid. He wants his father to see it.

"Whoa," his father says, and raises his hands. "Take it easy." He's talking to Fitz, but he's staring at the gun. "Slow down," he says. It's as if he's talking to the gun. He's transfixed. Fitz has wanted more than anything else in the world to get the man's attention and now, he's got it, undivided.

"You can have my wallet," his father says. "There's cash in it." He reaches slowly into his back pocket and produces a billfold. He holds it out to Fitz, a shiny black leather offering.

"Help yourself," his father says to the gun. "There's a hundred bucks, something like that." Fitz is still standing, leaning into the car, trying to use his body to shield the gun from the sight of anyone who may drive down the alley. Fitz grabs the wallet from his father. His father hands over his phone and Fitz snatches that, too. Under normal circumstances, he is a polite young man, no grabber, never was, but now it seems, hooded and armed in this alley, he is apparently someone else, someone other than who he thought he was.

It's a little disconcerting, hearing his father's voice. Fitz has heard it on his office voice mail—brisk and confident, away from his desk but eager to get back—and he's overheard him making small talk at a cash register—thank you, have a nice day. But now, directed at him, it's a different thing entirely.

"I don't want your money," Fitz tells him.

"You don't," his father says. "You don't want my money." Fitz expected his father to be something of a fast talker, but right now he is speaking very slowly, choosing his words carefully, the way a rock climber chooses his next step, slowly and deliberately, as if a single misstep would be deadly.

Fitz can imagine what his father must be thinking. The kid seems like he's on something. He's jumpy and nervous. He's sweating. It could be meth, the schools are full of it, he knows that, he reads the papers, kids getting high between classes, even in the suburban schools, especially the suburban schools.

The gun looks genuine. It's no water pistol, not a cap gun. He has no idea whether it's loaded. Maybe, maybe not. There's no way of telling. Fitz sees him still studying it.

"It's real," Fitz says.

"Of course it's real," his father says. "So is my money. But that's not what you want." He sounds irritated. Exasperated with this kid who doesn't seem to know how to conduct a proper holdup. Of all the muggers in the city, he gets the one who doesn't understand the object of the game. "What *do* you want?"

5

Fitz slides his backpack off his back, sets it on the floor of the car, and slips into the passenger seat. He holds the gun in front of him, not quite pointed at his father. When he imagined this, Fitz didn't consider he'd be so close, in such physical proximity. He can smell him—pungent and clean, his shower soap, his aftershave, some designer fragrance.

When he was very little, Fitz wanted more than anything to be close to his father. Like all kids, he learned at an early age to recognize and point to the daddies in his picture books—playing peekaboo with their little ones, giving them piggyback rides. He can't remember when he learned his family was different. At one point he started to call his beloved uncle Dunc, his mom's brother, "Daddy." It would have been an understandable mistake. It was Dunc who took him to the library, who peeled his apples, took him to breakfast on Saturday mornings, buttered his bagels and cut his pancakes and poured his syrup, who helped him in the bathroom, who roughhouse-wrestled with him when he came over, who let him strum the strings of his guitar as if he were playing.

But someone corrected him, set him straight. It was his mom. The tone of her voice let Fitz know that it was a serious mistake to call Dunc "Daddy." She didn't have to tell him twice. He learned to say "Uncle Dunc."

Fitz always understood that he had a father, but that his was elsewhere. He was "away"—that's how his mom put it. She was an expert dodger of his questions.

Where is he?

Away.

When is he coming home?

Soon.

Tomorrow? On my birthday?

We'll see.

Later he learned that his mother and father hadn't been married. He learned the name for a kid like him.

"Keep your hands on the wheel," Fitz tells his father. "Don't try anything."

His father obeys. He looks frightened, and Fitz doesn't mind. There's a weird power that comes with scaring someone, and right now Fitz is feeling it.

Mostly it wasn't so bad, he told himself. You get used to anything. It never felt tragic. Lots of kids had it worse. Fitz didn't feel entitled to feel sorry for himself. It wasn't like they were poor. He tried not to imagine what his life might be like if he had a dad. He thought if he did try, it might seem as if his mom wasn't great, which she was. But still. There was a hole. He didn't talk about it, but it was real.

Sometimes, it was just embarrassing. But over the years, Fitz developed various stratagems for handling father situations. When, for example, his friends' parents innocently ask, "What does your dad do?" he's learned to say quietly, "My dad's not with us anymore." He arranges his face into what he believes is an expression of respectful, wistful bereavement, and at those moments, he really does feel something like sadness for a father departed. "I'm so sorry," the adults inevitably say, a little flustered, and he forgives them their awkwardness, and they move on, and you can be certain that the topic of fathers does not come up again.

"Okay," Fitz tells his father. "Let's hit the road. Back the car out."

"The car?" his father says. "Is that what you want? Because you can have it. Be my guest."

"You think I want to jack your car?" Fitz says. "Is that what you think?"

"Tell me what you want," his father says. "Just say the word."

"Okay," Fitz says. "I'll tell you what I want. I'll say the word."

Fitz feels his heart beating in his chest. This is the time to say something, but what? He hasn't rehearsed this part. He has something to say, a little announcement to make, but he doesn't know the words. "What I want is to spend some time with you," he says at last. "You know, quality time. A little father-son time. Dad. That's the word."

Now his father is looking at him, not at his gun but right at him, as if for the first time. "Fitzgerald?" he says.

6

"*Listen, Fitzgerald,*" his father says. He's steering the car up Grand Avenue, away from downtown and his law offices, just as Fitz instructed. It's the first thing he's said since he figured out who Fitz was.

"Nobody calls me that," Fitz tells him. It's rush hour; traffic is heavy. There are people waiting at a bus shelter, drivers sipping from paper cups. Fitz glances at the clock on the dashboard: it's almost nine. On an ordinary day, he'd be in Mr. Massey's homeroom, probably listening to Caleb go on and on about some obscure bottleneck-guitar player from West Texas. But this is not an ordinary day. Fitz is still holding his gun, keeping it low, out of sight.

"I see," his father says. Fitz assumes he's making some calculations, thinking things through, trying to read the situation. This alleged son of his, this Fitzgerald person, what's the matter with him? Is he high? Crazy? He has no idea.

Fitz sees a coffee shop on the next block. It's his father's favorite—he's seen him carrying their cups. "Turn in there," he tells his father. "Get in the drive-through line. We'll get you some coffee."

His father does as he's told. There are a half dozen vehicles ahead of them in line, mostly SUVs, one nicely dressed person per car. Fitz thinks of his mom, how she likes to make fun of people who drink fancy overpriced coffee concoctions—the venti-soy-caramel-pumpkin-macchiato lattes, or whatever they are. The more complicated the order, the bigger the jerk—that's her theory. She used to be a waitress and knows all about customers and their orders. You can tell everything you need to know about a person, she says, just from watching how they behave in a restaurant, how they treat the help. When the two of them go out, his mom tips crazy amounts—the grubbier the place, the more she leaves—because she knows what it's like.

When they pull up to the speaker, Fitz hides the gun under his sweatshirt. His father rolls his window down. He glances at Fitz. "And what about you?" his father asks. "What would you like?"

"Hot chocolate," Fitz says, without thinking. The words just jump out of his mouth. It's what he wants, what he gets at a place like this, but he hasn't thought about how it might sound, what it would look like. The little gangster sipping his cocoa. He watches his father's face and thinks, *Don't laugh at me, don't you dare laugh at me*. He'd rather his father shoot him than laugh at him.

His father's face shows nothing. If he's amused, he keeps it to himself. He leans into the speaker and places their order. Fitz notices that his father is pleasant and polite. The girl has to interrupt him and ask him to wait a minute. Then she mishears him and he has to repeat himself, twice. She's having a hard time, but he's the one who apologizes. He thanks her for taking his order. It surprises Fitz a little. Especially now, under the circumstances. Because he wears a suit, maybe, because he seems like a boss, Fitz has imagined his father ordering people around at work, being abrupt with underlings. But he doesn't bark at the girl. He's gracious. His mom would give him points for that. He has good manners, he is capable of kindness.

And yet, somehow even this, especially this, bugs Fitz. The man can be nice to a stranger, a voice on a speaker, but he ignores his son? All these years, what prevented his father from being nice to *him*? Why didn't he knock on the door? Why didn't he pick up the phone and call? Why didn't he write a letter? Why? Why? Why? It is the central mystery of his life. The unanswerable question. Fitz did not agonize over the existence of God; he didn't ponder the origins of the universe. Sometimes he would look at himself in the mirror, an expression of pathetic eagerness on his face. He was a dog in the pound, wanting to be adopted. He'd smile. What father wouldn't want this boy?

They edge toward the window. "So what do they call you?" his father asks, his eyes straight ahead.

"Huh?"

"If not Fitzgerald. You said nobody calls you that. You must have a nickname or something. What *do* they call you?"

"Orphan Boy," Fitz says. "That's my handle."

Fitz isn't sure where it's coming from, this attitude, this hostility, whatever it is he's channeling, exactly. It's like he's possessed by something, speaking in evil tongues. Normally, he's respectful to adults. His ordinary, everyday self makes eye contact and never

23

interrupts or mouths off—usually he's a regular please-and-thank-you machine. A pleasure to have in class, that's the box all his teachers check. Maybe he's trying to make up for the hot chocolate, proving he's still a tough guy. Maybe he's tapped a deep well of something black and nasty, like some underground oil deposit, buried deep in his soul.

"What right have you got to even say my name?" Fitz says. "Tell me that."

"None. None whatsoever." His father raises his hands off the steering wheel then, and Fitz tenses, but it's not an attack, just a gesture, a mini-surrender: he shows his palms and returns them to the wheel.

At the window now, there's a perky blond girl wearing a headset and an apron who tells them what they owe. Fitz remembers that he's got his father's billfold jammed in his hip pocket. He pulls it out and extracts a ten. He gives it to his father, who thanks him and passes it up to the girl.

She makes change and hands it to his father, who in turn passes it to Fitz. She hands over their drinks next, two tall, lidded paper cups. His father sets his in the console's cup holder between them.

The girl gives them a big smile and tells them to enjoy their day. Maybe she imagines the two of them are on some nice family outing, Take Your Son to Work Day or some such.

Which reminds Fitz. "You need to call your office," he says. He's thought this through and has a kind of outline in his head, but he's let himself get flustered and forgetful. He needs to get back on track. He needs to stay focused. "Tell them you're not coming in today."

"They're gonna want to know why."

He pulls his father's phone out of his pocket and thrusts it at him. "Tell 'em you're sick," Fitz says. There's a word his mom likes. "Tell 'em you're *indisposed*. Tell 'em whatever you like. I don't care. Tell 'em you have plans."

"Because you have plans for me," his father says. "Is that right?"

"Oh yes," Fitz tells him. "Most definitely. I have plans. Big plans."

7

Fitz has always been fascinated by fathers—the various types, their behaviors. When he visits his friends, he studies their dads, like a zoologist doing field research. He likes to catalog the various species he observes. There are the lawn-and-garden dads, guys who smell like gasoline, who spend the weekends mowing and edging, blowing leaves and whacking weeds. There are hunters and fishermen, the ones with camo jackets and tackle boxes, boat hitches on their trucks. There are the sports guys, coaches and superfans, sitting on the sidelines in their portable chairs, hollering encouragement and advice. Dads read the paper; they grill meat; they pay bills. They drink beer and watch football, remotes glued to their hands. That's how they are on television anyway. Most TV dads are a little clueless, big kids. Bad dads turn up mostly in movies and lit class: the Great Santini, Huck's dad—they're angry and mean and sometimes drunk.

But this man at the wheel, his dad, is not so easy to classify. He's got his eyes on the road, headed down Lexington Avenue now, just as Fitz instructed him, toward Como Park. If he is a bad dad—of course he is!—it is a different kind of bad. He is quietly, almost invisibly, bad. If he were a disease, they'd call him a silent killer.

Now that phrase, it occurs to Fitz, could make a good blues song: *You're a silent killer, baby.* It's crazy to be thinking about songs now, in the front seat with his dad, his hand on a gun, but it's just how his mind works—he can't help himself. He thinks up a good phrase, hears some choice expression, he wants to write it down, fiddle around with it, see if it turns into anything worth showing Caleb.

Fitz wishes Caleb could be here with him. Caleb is peculiar and superstitious, full of tics and rituals and crazy fears—there are certain streets he doesn't like to cross, some chords he seems to dread—but he's shrewd, too. He sees into people. Caleb would have some take on his father. He could help Fitz see beyond the briefcase and cell phone, help him see what's in the suit.

What's he listen to? That's what Caleb would want to know. When he talks, Caleb puts a little spin on certain words—it's like he speaks in italics. He can be so serious sometimes, people think he must be joking. But Fitz understands. That's what makes him Caleb. *Check out the man's music,* Caleb would tell him.

Fitz looks around and finds a wallet of CDs above the visor. He takes it down and flips through it. On top is *Rubber Soul.* It's a record that Fitz owns and has listened to for years: the Beatles are one of the bands Fitz and his mom agree on. The Beatles—that's their common ground.

They stop at a red light, and Fitz's father glances over at him. "So what do you have in mind? The park?" He looks worried.

He probably thinks Fitz is going to shoot him there and leave his body in the shrubbery for some jogger to discover. Like something from a mob movie, some poor loser gets driven to a desolate location and then whacked. Fine, Fitz thinks. Let him stew. Let his lousy life pass before his eyes.

But what Fitz has in mind is a different kind of movie, a movie he's been watching in his head. In this movie, there's no dialogue, just Fitz and his father together, doing things. It's a montage, snippets and glimpses of a shared life. They're fishing; they're washing a car; they're shooting hoops. Some of the images don't even make sense, at least not for Fitz—he's never had any special love of basketball, for one thing. Maybe it's just the best his imagination can do: probably these are scenes he's cribbed from the movies or other kids' lives. Somehow the particulars don't seem to matter all that much. What matters is getting what he's owed.

A year ago, Fitz's mom received a good-sized check from the school where she works as a teacher's aide: it was to make up for a pay raise she was supposed to have gotten months before. Instead of getting a little bit every two weeks, she got it all at once, a big lump of money. Back pay, that's what it was. Maybe that's what Fitz wants: a lump sum of his father's time and attention. Back pay.

"First, we're gonna check out the zoo," Fitz says.

"Sure," his father says. "Check out the zoo."

Maybe his father thinks he's kidding, but he's not. The zoo is one of his favorite places in the world. His mom used to take Fitz to the Como Zoo all the time when he was little, probably because it was free. There were animals there he grew to love—the sea lions, the bison, all the cats, especially the snow leopard. He loved the animals not as species but as individuals—*that* gorilla, the young male, the shy one; Buzz, the polar bear, and his brother, Neil. He didn't just love the charismatic mammals: he loved amphibians and reptiles, too, he loved animals that were scaly and prickly, bug-eyed and menacing. Animals other kids thought were gross or uninteresting, the sloth, say, Fitz thought were simply misunderstood, as deserving of fans as their cuter fellow creatures.

"The zoo even open today?"

Fitz is still holding the CD wallet. He flips through to see what else his father listens to: the Clash, Dinah Washington, Lucinda Williams, Wilco, the Replacements, Bob Marley.

"I'm in a band, you know," Fitz says.

"Really," his father says.

"Really."

"What's it called?"

"Creative Destruction." Fitz and Caleb went around and around trying to come up with a name. At one point, they had more than a hundred possibilities. Creative Destruction was something Fitz heard on the radio. He didn't know what it meant, but he liked the sound of it. Caleb had been holding out for Osgood-Schlatter, which is a disease but sounds like a person. Nora Flynn was with them after school that day in the commons. They'd been trying to recruit her to sing with them, so when she said she liked "Creative Destruction," that sealed it.

"Cool," his father says. Fitz looks at him. Is he humoring him? Being smart? Yanking his chain—like Dominic at the playground? Fitz has no idea. He can't read him. He regrets telling him that much.

"Yeah," Fitz says. "Groovy."

Fitz wonders if his father even likes his music all that much. Probably these CDs are just fashionable props, like his briefcase, a bunch of titles recommended in some slick men's magazine.

Fitz slides the Dinah Washington out of its sleeve. He's heard the name, probably from Caleb, the music encyclopedia. He slips it into the player, and the first track starts just as they see the first sign for the zoo. There's some strings, then Dinah starts singing, belting it out in this amazing voice: "What a difference a day makes/Twenty-four little hours."

8

"*Pull over,*" Fitz tells his father.

They're on the park grounds now, just passing the Frog Pond. Fitz can see the dome of the conservatory, a huge, humid green-house full of exotic flowers, shrubs, ferns, and even trees. Fitz thinks of his mom—the Como Conservatory is one of her favorite places in the world. They've been visiting together for years: even if they come to the park for the animals or the rides, they usually stop in at least, pay a quick visit. She loves it, and he endures it for her sake. She can look at orchids forever, and Fitz sort of understands—here, she is like how he and Caleb are at the music store. If you know the stuff, flowers or guitars, it doesn't matter, if you love them, they are all fascinating and beautiful, the colors and shapes and smells of them. He and his mom usually talk a little about what they're looking at, take turns playing the teacher, so now his mom knows the difference between a Les Paul and a Strat, and Fitz has learned some basic flower names. Fitz has, though he would never admit it, grown especially fond of the crooked little bonsais, the Japanese trees in pots, which seem to him to have distinctive personalities, some of them looking feisty and defiant, others sad and apologetic.

Where does a guy like his father go to lose himself? Fitz wonders. What does he look at to cheer himself up? What makes his tail wag? Sports cars, maybe? Italian suits? Fancy watches? Fitz has no idea.

His father slows the car down a little, but he doesn't stop.

"I said, pull over." Fitz raises the gun again. "Now." His father covers the brake, checks his mirror, and parks at the curb. He glances at Fitz then, as if for his approval: Fitz feels like the most hard-core driving instructor in the history of the world. The gun, it occurs to Fitz, is just like the conch, the shell that the wild pack of boys in *Lord of the Flies* uses in their councils—as long as you're holding it, people listen to you. Fitz holds it now, and he's not about to let it go.

"Okay," Fitz says. "Turn the car off and hand me the keys."

His father obeys. He takes the keys from the ignition and holds them out in the palm of his hand. Fitz grabs them and pockets them with his left hand, the gun in his right hand, at his hip.

His father is looking at Fitz now in a way that seems almost clinical, studying him, as if Fitz is a client or even a patient—he's silently taking him in, taking his measure, forming some kind of judgment or diagnosis.

"So," his father says. "What's your favorite subject?" He sounds like a school nurse making small talk while she's preparing to take out a sliver, that same tone of voice, kindly in a sort of abstracted, generic way. It's how you talk if you get paid to be nice, if you don't want to scare someone you know you're going to hurt.

32

"You're kidding me, right?" Fitz says. "What's my favorite subject?"

"I'm just asking."

Fitz feels another wave of anger wash over him. His father's composure, his professional cool, his small talk, here and now, with a gun in his face—it's making him crazy. "What was yours? Life-wrecking? Is that a subject? I'm just asking."

His father leans away from Fitz, away from the heat of his outburst. It's how people respond to the scarily inappropriate. It's the posture of *whoa, where's that coming from?*

But Fitz doesn't feel like backing off. "You wanna bond now?" he asks. "Is that the idea?"

"It's never too late," his father says.

"Really?" Fitz says. "Is that what you think? You sure about that? Never too late? Really? Never? *Never?*"

His father says nothing. His lips twitch and retract a little—it's the beginnings of a smile or a smirk. He shows his perfect teeth.

Fitz feels the sweaty weight of the gun in his hand. "What if I knock that stupid grin off your face?" Fitz says. He raises his left hand, a tight fist now, as if to deliver a backhanded blow. His father flinches.

"We're bonding now," Fitz says. "Don't you think? We're bonding like crazy. We're having us some special times, wouldn't you say so?"

His father's hair is messed up now. There's a swatch that's come unmoussed from the top of his head. It's sticking up, like a little shaft of wheat. He exhales. It was a scared and nervous smile, Fitz realizes.

"I understand why you hate me," his father says quietly. "I get it."

"Out of the car," Fitz tells him. He doesn't want to have this conversation. Being understood is not on the agenda, not now, not by this guy.

They step out and slam their doors at the same time. It's like they're a couple of cops on a call. Behind the conservatory, the zoo itself is out of sight, but Fitz can smell it, that familiar animal smell. Fitz can hear what sounds like a mower in the distance, but there's no one around. After some rain the week before, the grass is greening up nicely. The yellow heads of dandelions are popping up.

Fitz thinks he should maybe lock the car, but he doesn't want to have to fish in his pocket for the keys and mess around with the buttons. He steps around the back of the car, comes up on the driver's side, and stops just a couple of paces from his father.

"Let's go for a walk," Fitz says. He motions with his gun. He looks over his shoulder—there's no one in sight.

Fitz sees his father glance at his suit coat hanging in the back of the car, his briefcase resting on the seat.

"You're not going to need that," Fitz says.

"Sure," his father says. "Of course not." He stands there, looking awkward, waggling his arms a little, sneaking another glance toward the backseat.

Fitz realizes that his father must feel naked—without his phone, his keys, his wallet, without his standard props, his usual gear, without his suit jacket and briefcase. Fitz imagines going further: making him take off his watch, his silk tie, his crisp white shirt. He imagines stripping him to his shorts, leaving him to wander the park grounds in his boxers. Would he even know who he was?

"Come on," Fitz tells him. "Forward march."

Fitz directs his father to head back on the access road toward the Frog Pond. They walk, and Fitz thinks about what his father told him in the car. *I understand why you hate me.* It bothers him. *Hate* is just not a word Fitz would usually associate with himself.

During Spirit Week at school, they were supposed to work up a rabid hatred for their oldest football rival. There were slogans and posters and a lumpy dummy wearing their opponents' jersey hanging in the commons that kids would elbow as they walked by. As if the other guys were real enemies and not just kids like them who happened to live in a different district. It was stupid and a little frightening. In Mr. Massey's class, they'd been reading *1984*, but no one else seemed to make the connection. It was just like Hate Week. Same thing exactly. At the Friday pep rally, everyone got all whipped up, even the teachers, especially the teachers. Fitz remembers looking around and seeing Mr. Weber, a harmless, chalk-stained guy who taught geometry, King of the Sweater Vest—his face was all red from shouting, he was inflamed with it, he was on fire. At the time, Fitz judged Mr. Weber: to be so hateful was unattractive. Fitz must have thought he was somehow exempt from that kind of thing, above it.

"Walk toward the water," Fitz tells his father, and he does as he's told. Steps over the curb onto the grass, walks along at a nice clip, not too fast, not too slow, Fitz following behind, his eyes on the back of his father's head, the gun now tucked in the pouch of his sweatshirt. If his father takes off running, if he makes a break for it, Fitz wonders, can he pull the trigger? Does he have it in him?

They stop at the water's edge, under the cover of a couple of trees. It would be a good spot for a picnic. There are little ripples in the water, fish coming up to the surface to feed on insects. Fitz can see the granite bullfrog in the middle of the pond, sitting on his concrete slab, looking, as he always does to him, Buddha-like, serenely calm and self-contained. Fitz used to skip rocks at him. Now the bullfrog looks on, a silent witness to the drama being played out in front of him: a boy, a gun, and a man, two wildly beating human hearts.

They stand together for a moment, not speaking, hypnotized a little maybe by the water, feeling it, thinking their own thoughts. And then his father makes a slow pivot with his shiny black shoe, starts to execute an about-face.

"Don't," Fitz tells him. "Don't turn around. I don't want to see your face." He takes the gun from his sweatshirt.

"It doesn't have to be this way," his father says. "We should have talked a long time ago. I know. It's all my fault. I don't know if I can make it up to you. But I can try. Let me try. Give me a chance. That's all I'm asking. A chance."

The possibility that now—now!—his father might be offering what he's longed for his whole life—it's too much to bear. It's not to be endured. Fitz has heard that a starving man offered a big meal will choke on it. What you most need, too much, too late, it could kill you. It makes perfect sense to Fitz. Of course.

"I promise," his father says. "I swear to God."

Promise? What good is a promise made at gunpoint? Fitz knows if they're scared enough, if they're terrified, people will confess to anything, promise anything.

"Shut it," Fitz says. "Shut your lying mouth."

"Hurting me," his father says, "isn't going to make you feel any better, Fitzgerald."

Now, now Fitz feels it, the real thing, no rah-rah, pep rally synthetic. The genuine article. Hate. He can feel it, he can practically hear it sizzling in his blood. He hates his father's know-it-all psychology. He hates his white shirt and the smell of his cologne. He hates that he is still calling him Fitzgerald, and he hates that even now, he's still talking, still pleading, still litigating. And deep down, probably, Fitz knows his father is right, and that makes him hate him even more.

"Shut up," Fitz says.

"Listen," his father says.

"I don't want to listen to you." Fitz raises his arm and points the gun at his father's head. "I want you to shut up."

Fitz can imagine it. Not just see it but feel it. A loud report, the gun's kickback, this man crumpling, blood on his beautiful white shirt.

It sickens him. He's always been squeamish. Blood, cuts, wounds, his own or in movies, it turns his stomach. He has to look away. In his whole life, Fitz has been in all of one fight, a stupid altercation over a *Pokémon* card with a kid from down the street, and when Stuey first shoved and then punched him in the stomach, he hardly fought back—the kid was an idiot, but Fitz didn't want to hurt him.

Killer instinct? He doesn't have it. As an assassin, he's a complete failure.

"Bang," Fitz hears himself say. "Bang-bang."

9

The world seems to resume now, at full speed. For a moment, it slowed and then stopped. Fitz has almost done something, but the world hasn't noticed. Fish are still feeding in the pond. The lawn mower is still rumbling in the distance. There's a woodpecker somewhere jackhammering a tree. The Buddha-bullfrog is still looking on.

His father has turned around, and Fitz is down now, on one knee. He can't remember dropping, but here he is, kneeling. It feels like a good, solid position. He feels anchored, grounded. The gun is still in his hand, he's lowered it, but it's at his side, pointed down.

His heart is pounding, his hair is wet with sweat, but he feels better somehow. He feels as if he's thrown up, emptied himself, expelled something poisonous. The heat of his hatred seems to have been short-lived, a two-minute hate at best.

What comes next? Fitz thinks. After hate?

When it occurs to Fitz that this could be the germ of a song ("What comes after the hate?/Something something too late?"), that's when he realizes he must be okay. The demon who possessed him must have departed, he understands, left him, like a fever, sweating and weak and a little disoriented but restored. He is himself again.

"Okay," his father says. His tie is askew, his belt buckle off-center. He makes a cautious palms-out gesture, just the way you show a strange dog you mean no harm. He looks vulnerable, defenseless, he looks suddenly unarmed, unprotected, un-everythinged.

Something has passed between them, they've shared something, whatever it is, something that can never be put into words. Fitz knows he will never really write a song about it. There's no word for what just happened, and nothing rhymes with it.

"So," his father says. He looks as if he's aged somehow from the time he stepped out of his building, lost some of that youthful buoyancy. He doesn't look like a tennis champion now. He doesn't look like an ace litigator. He looks like, like what?

"So," his father says again. "Now what?"

A TALE OF LOVE AND WAR

"*So, Curtis,*" *Fitz says*. It's easier than he thought to call his father by his first name. But why not? It's a little late to be worrying about social niceties. "You're not grossed out, are you?"

They're holding paper cones full of diced fish parts. Below them is a rowdy pack of sea lions jostling each other, trying to establish a position, barking up at them.

Back at the Frog Pond, they reached an understanding. Fitz agreed to put the gun away, his father promised to be an agreeable companion, no back talk. No shooting, no bolting, that's their deal.

"No," his father says. "I'm not grossed out." He's unbuttoned the cuffs of his shirt and turned up the sleeves and has been looking into his cup. It is a smelly, fish-flavor snow cone, full of scaly chunks, some eyeballs, too. He gives it a little shake. But he hasn't picked up anything yet.

Fitz has already tossed off almost half of his, aiming for one sea lion in particular on the periphery, a teenager, Fitz imagines, not so fat, a little less pushy. So far Fitz has made two successful long throws that have carried over the main gang and landed directly in this fellow's mouth. Fitz feels a connection with him, like they're buddies, a kind of team.

Now, finally, his father reaches into his cup, boldly grabs a big piece, as if to show how not grossed out he is. He tosses it off with a certain jaunty style, backhanded, with a flick of his wrist, like a Frisbee.

Fitz has always loved the sea lions. He loves their speed, their unapologetic appetite, their slickness, their capacity for mischief. He can't prove it—and he knows a zoologist would probably scoff—but Fitz is convinced some animals have a sense of humor. Not giraffes—too nervous—not sloths or boars—too sluggish and slow-witted—but lemurs, say, otters for sure, and sea lions.

The zoo is still pretty quiet. They're nearly the only ones around. In an hour or so, the school field-trip kids will be here, with their name tags and bag lunches, getting herded from exhibit to exhibit. But now, it is basically just the two of them and a few khaki keepers sweeping and hosing, one sleepy-looking guy picking up garbage with a sharp stick, a few gulls perched on the ledge of the sea lion enclosure, eyeing the fish but keeping their distance. Fitz and his father are out in the open, in public, but they're alone, too. It feels private. It's the kind of time and place that spies in movies meet to exchange their secrets.

"Okay," his father says, "okay, big guy. You next." He is talking to the most boisterous sea lion, who is sitting on the rocks directly beneath them, yapping up at them, head tilted back, looking like a goofy earless dog.

"All right," his father says. "Here you go—a nice juicy piece."

Fitz and his mom always talk to the animals, and sometimes his mom makes them talk back. She's got a whole repertoire of cartoonish voices: squeaky and manic for the monkeys, deep and ponderous for the elephants.

Fitz almost talks back to his father in his mom's gruff and gargoylish sea lion voice—"Thank you, friend, much obliged"—but catches himself just in time.

Did they ever go to the zoo together? Fitz wonders. Young Annie McGrath and Curtis Powell? He can't quite picture it. His mom and this guy, the two of them a happy couple, smiling, holding hands maybe. But that doesn't mean it didn't happen. No matter what, it pleases Fitz that his father is talking to the sea lions. Maybe it's a good sign.

His father is leaning on the wall of the enclosure, resting on his elbows. "Where to begin," his father says. He is looking down at the sea lions, but now he is talking to Fitz.

Fitz doesn't know what he's supposed to say. *Begin at the beginning*—that sounds stupid.

"I don't know how much you know," his father says. "I don't know how much she's told you."

"She?"

"Your mother," his father says. "Annie."

"What's to tell?" Fitz says. "You knocked her up. You couldn't be bothered. A kid wasn't on the agenda. You had other plans. So you were, like, goodbye, good luck, check's in the mail."

"That's what she told you?"

Actually, it isn't. Not at all. It's more like the story he's been telling himself lately. At least it is a story. Maybe it's miserable, but at least it makes some sense. It's something solid, something you could hold on to. What his mom gave him wasn't even a story. It was something else. A puzzle, a mystery, a crime scene.

From his mom he never got a straight story. Over the years, he's tried, really tried, to get some answers. His dad's last name— he learned that from the return address on an envelope when he was maybe eight years old. There was something about it that made him think it was special. The way his mom took it out of the mailbox and quickly slipped it into her purse, where he found it and studied it when she was out of the room. It came from Missouri. The printing on the envelope was precise. "Who's Powell?" he asked her that night at dinner. "It's my dad, right?" Somehow he just knew. She wouldn't tell him much else. Why was he writing? Business. Was it about him? No. Was he coming to visit? No. He found another letter in the mailbox a couple of years later and held it up to the light. It was a check. By then he understood about child support. What he didn't understand was why his dad would pay for him but not visit him.

What happened? Who was his father, really? How did she feel about him? How did he land outside his dad's reach?

He could never get his mom to budge beyond her standard spiel. Once, when Fitz was pestering her about the possibility that his dad might be famous—a rock star, say, or a professional athlete—she admitted that he was a lawyer. But mostly, it was dial-a-cliché. They were just kids back then, she told him once, young and foolish, babies, how could it last, it wasn't meant to be, his father was a good man who always wanted what was best for Fitz.

When Fitz tried to follow up—when he asked why, for example, if his father was such a good man, he didn't come around—she'd smile, a little sadly, and stonewall, patient as an all-day rain, shut the door with some evasion or non sequitur. "He's in St. Louis," she said once, as if that explained everything. St. Louis, where good men are kept from their kids. Or she'd give him some pseudo-profound, fortune-cookie philosophy: "Love is a crooked road." Finally, as a last resort, when all else failed, she'd flip into monster-mom mode, start grooming him, straightening his collar, spit on her finger and mess with his hair, and tell him what a fine young man he was, how proud she was of him.

So he was left with only hints, echoes and glimpses, scraps and shards.

Her books, for example. She was just now about to graduate from college, cramming four years of higher education into twelve, she liked to joke, taking a night class for as long as Fitz could remember, lugging one fat textbook or another around with her yellow highlighter. But beyond that, besides her studying, she was always reading, not for school, just for fun, for pleasure. Mostly paperbacks she scooped up at garage sales and then lined up on the cinder-block shelves in her bedroom—so many books, Fitz had a hard time believing she'd read all of them. He used to quiz her. Who wrote *East of Eden? Death Comes for the Archbishop?* She always knew.

There were a bunch of books on her shelf by F. Scott Fitzgerald, his namesake, of course. In February, when Mr. Massey assigned *The Great Gatsby* in English 10, Fitz read her copy. The stuff she'd underlined made him wonder. Nothing that would help you on a quiz, just random words and phrases: "wild unknown men," "warm human magic," "purposeless splendor," "I hate careless people," "tragic arguments," "a decade of loneliness," "his ghostly heart." It was like some kind of coded message, a secret story.

And then, in one of her books, A *Farewell to Arms*, a book she seemed to be reading for about the third time, Fitz found something. On the inside cover, written in neat blue printing: *Powell*. So, one of her books, one of her *favorite* books—"a tender tale of love and war," the back cover called it—had his name in it. She never returned it, never threw it out. She kept reading it, again and again. That meant something. But what?

Fitz has tried to solve it himself, piece it all together. Figure out how he fits in. Build it himself—the skeleton of his parents' lives. Play *CSI: Mom and Dad*. He's tried and tried and tried and never cracked the case. He is a lousy investigator.

"She hasn't told me very much at all," Fitz says. "Not really." He feels like he should be saying something more combative, something provocative. Maintain the attitude, keep playing the role of his father's worst nightmare. But it's getting harder to do.

Fitz's meanness this day, the real nastiness, has been a little like a presentation or a speech, something he's been working on for a while, something rehearsed and recited. It's been aimed at the guy on the law firm's website, aimed at the guy who lives in a big apartment and drives a fancy car, aimed at the idea of his father. But in front of him now is no idea—it is a real man. His father doesn't look much like his picture now. He's got some gray hairs at the temple, a worried crease in his forehead. Fitz feels like he's losing his bad-guy script now, forgetting his lines.

"Practically nothing," he says. "That's what she told me."

"Did she tell you who was in the delivery room when you were born?" his father asks. He straightens up now, stands and turns toward Fitz. "Did she tell you who cut the cord? The first face you ever saw? Did she tell you who that was?"

Fitz looks down. His paper cup is empty. His hands stink. The sea lions have moved on—they're in the pool, dipping and diving, doing what looks like the backstroke. He envies them. Suddenly what Fitz wants more than anything else is to wash his hands.

11

CERTIFICATE OF LIVE BIRTH. That's what it said on the top. That there was another kind of birth was not something he wanted to think about.

The first time he knew there was such a thing as a birth certificate was when his mom needed to bring a copy to his peewee soccer coach as evidence that he really was eight years old. He can't remember thinking much about it one way or the other. It was just an official piece of paper, something to be handed in, like a permission slip.

But six months ago, when he needed the birth certificate to register for driver's ed, he got real interested in it. In social studies, they were always doing DBQs—document-based questions. This was the real thing, an actual document, only this one wasn't about the Great Depression or the Civil War. It was about him.

It came at a weird time for Fitz. He'd been in to the guidance counselor's office just a couple of days before. She wanted to get acquainted. "What makes you tick?" she asked with a big smile.

"What are you all about?" Ms. Perkins was cool. Everyone loved her. She wasn't trying to put him on the spot. She just wanted to get to know him. But he was flummoxed. He came up empty, drew a blank. Everyone else seemed to have some kind of signature style, some brand. He got red in the face. He stared at his shoes. He managed to say something, finally, stuttered something out, and she took some notes.

What was he all about? He had no idea. He was no athlete. He studied but really wasn't a great student. He played music, but he wasn't a musician, not like Caleb, not a singer like Nora. He wasn't an outlaw or rebel, not that things didn't bother him—but he didn't act or protest, more out of inertia. When Ms. Perkins left the room to get some literature about a test she thought he ought to take, he looked at her notes. *Seems somewhat adrift.* That's what she'd written. It was terrible, because it felt true. It described perfectly how it felt to be him—drifting, floating away, no anchor, no control, no destination.

That night he put some questions into a search engine: *What's wrong with me? What makes me tick?* He felt crazy and ashamed doing it, but curious, too. But it didn't help. He still felt indistinct, somehow, blank, undifferentiated. He couldn't help but feel that it was connected to his father's absence. That hole he felt but never talked about. He couldn't help but blame this guy.

On the birth certificate there was his full name written out: *Fitzgerald John McGrath.* Fitzgerald John, like the president, only backward, which was clever, Fitzgerald for his mom's favorite writer, John for her dad.

For something like thirty years, his grandfather worked at the Ford plant in St. Paul, "on the line," he used to say, though Fitz was never quite sure what that meant. One thing it meant was that they always drove Fords. Uncle Dunc is still driving a ten-year-old Crown Vic. His mom drives a Focus now because of her dad. He died years earlier, when Fitz was six, after a short and horrible descent into cancer. Fitz remembers him, at their dining room table, looking shrunken and scared, staring at a heaping plate his mom prepared for him—as if you could cure cancer with mashed potatoes and gravy—and looking at his favorite food as if it was something he'd never seen before, something completely strange and foreign.

But Fitz remembers him best with his tools and gear, working on some household project his mom assigned him: installing a ceiling fan, putting a new roof on the garage, building shelves for his bedroom. When he was really little, Fitz just trailed after him, watched, toting his own plastic tools.

Fitz loved it when his grandfather would stop, put down his tools, and announce that it was time for a coffee break. They'd sit together at the kitchen table, a plate of his mom's homemade cookies between them, usually big, chewy molasses cookies, which were his grandpa's favorite. Coffee for his grandpa, milk for Fitz. Fitz learned from his grandpa to dunk his cookies, a habit his mom pretended to think was disgusting, and her disapproval made it even more enjoyable. Fitz missed those times with his grandpa. He kept his hammer in his room—it was better than a photograph—and when he needed to write out his full name, it made him happy to write out *John*; it pleased him to see it on his birth certificate.

He wanted to believe that there might be something of his grand-father in him—his patient skill maybe, his ingenuity.

His dad's full name was on the birth certificate, too: Curtis Ward Powell. With that, he was able to find him. There's a lot of Curtis Powells in the world but only one with that name practic-ing law.

More than once his mom has told Fitz about his birth: he was in a big hurry to come into the world. That was the theme of the story as she told it. She had a few contractions, drove to the hos-pital, and then, practically before they could get her wheeled into the delivery room and the doctor was suited up, there he was. That's what she told him. According to his mom, he's always been that way—eager, in a hurry.

There's a photograph taken on the day he was born. It's in a little wood frame and has been on the top of his mom's dresser for as long as Fitz can remember. In the picture, he—Baby Fitz—is wearing a miniature knit cap adorned with a little blue ribbon. It's very stylish, Fitz has always thought, a good look. He wishes he still looked that good in a hat, but he just doesn't.

His face is red and scrunched, but his baby eyes are open—deep blue pools taking in this big strange world. His head is being held up, of course, supported. In the margins of the picture you can see a little bit of the forearm of the person who is holding him. And who *is* holding him?

He's never really thought about whose arm, no more than he ever considered who framed the picture or who put the little hat on his head—it never crossed his mind. But it's clearly a man's arm, muscular and covered with dark hair. Before today, if he'd been asked, if it was a question on some crazy test about himself, he'd have said Grandpa John. Or Uncle Dunc, or maybe a nurse, some hospital aide.

It could be his father in the picture. It's possible. What he said. That he was there that day, in the delivery room, when Fitz made his famous fast entry into the world.

But so what? If his mom's story was not the whole truth? If the mystery arm belonged to his father? What then? Would it even matter?

12

Fitz looks at his father's arms, his hands. They're sitting on a bench across from what is going to be a new polar bear habitat. Fitz and his father have been to the men's room and have washed up. In the dark mirror of the zoo's bathroom, Fitz's reflection didn't look quite like himself. He looked scared and menacing, slightly crazed.

Fitz bought a bottle of water for each of them from a vending machine. He's not really thirsty, but it gives them something to do. They sip, they spin the bottles in their hands, they look at the labels. His mom is all about proper hydration, she would approve.

Fitz tells his father that if anyone was at the hospital the day he was born, he always thought it was his Grandpa John.

"He never liked me," his father says.

"Why not?"

"He was not an easy man," he says. Fitz knows his grandpa used to be a drinker. He quit—"put the cork in the bottle," that's how he put it—when Fitz was little. Fitz has no real memories of him drunk or drinking. He was a Pepsi fiend, that's what

Fitz remembers, knocking back bottle after bottle, bringing it home by the case. But his mom and uncle have stories about his temper.

"Plus I drove a foreign car," his father says. "That was unforgivable. And I didn't know the difference between a manifold and a master cylinder."

Fitz doesn't know much about cars either. He and his mom change the oil in her car but that's about it.

"I couldn't fix things. I was a college boy."

"He always told me I had to go to college," Fitz says. "So I wouldn't have to work in a factory. He and my mom, 'College, college, college.' "

"That's different," his father says. "You were his grandson. I was the guy who, you know, like you said. His little girl."

"His only daughter."

"Exactly." He looks up, surprised a little, Fitz thinks, maybe even grateful, that he gets it, that he knows how to fill in the blanks.

"But the day you were born, he was on his best behavior. I have to give him that. He didn't say much. But he didn't have to. He had a look. It made me feel like a bug. You probably never saw that look."

In the polar bear exhibit there's some serious earth-moving equipment rumbling behind the line of fencing. A sign explains that Buzz and Neil are on loan somewhere. Fitz is glad they're getting a new and improved home. It used to make him sad to see them pacing and swimming figure eights in their tiny pool. "Get me out of here," his mom said once as they watched, using her slow and deep polar bear voice, sounding so weary and defeated it just about broke Fitz's heart.

"But you were there, in the hospital?" he asks.

"In the hospital. In the delivery room."

"My mom says I was fast. In a hurry. That I made a quick entrance."

"Oh yes. You sure did. You most definitely did." His father takes a sip of water and looks off. To Fitz, his father looks as if he's remembering something, feeling something. But how can he be sure? The man is a lawyer. He is a professional persuader. He's good at it. There's no way to know if he's being sincere or just acting.

Fitz decides to plow ahead anyway. "There's a picture of me," he says. "My face is all scrunched up. I'm wearing a little cap thing."

"With a blue ribbon on it."

"You know that picture."

"I know it."

"Someone's holding me in that picture. You can see his hands."

His father sets his bottle of water on the ground. He holds his hands out in front of him, palms up. Just the way you would cradle a newborn, his long fingers extended, his right hand raised slightly to support the head. Except that his hands are empty. Fitz and his father stare into those empty hands, hands holding nothing, holding an invisible baby, holding the baby that Fitz used to be. Fitz can almost, but not quite, see his baby self.

Those hands, his father's empty hands—they may be the saddest thing Fitz has ever seen. But for the first time today, the first time ever, Fitz knows it—he feels it. This is his father.

13

They're still sitting on their bench. The sun is higher in the sky now. It's warming up. If Fitz didn't have a gun stuck in his waistband, he'd think about pulling off his sweatshirt. His father has picked up his bottle of water, and they've each been sipping, listening to the growl and whine of construction, thinking their own thoughts.

"She says you were young and foolish," Fitz says at last. "Young and foolish. Like it was the name of a soap opera."

"The Young and the Foolish."

"Were you?"

"Oh yes," his father says. "*I* was. I'll speak for myself. I had a starring role in that show."

Fitz wants more but isn't quite sure how to draw it out. He knows that stories can be cautious animals, like chipmunks or rabbits, and Fitz doesn't want to scare this one away. He decides just to hold still, wait.

"It's none of my business, I know," his father says. "I have no right to ask. But I wonder if you have a girl. You don't have to answer."

Fitz thinks about Nora. He actually had a conversation with her after school the day before. Supposedly about singing in the band now that the spring musical was done. He didn't tell her that whenever he heard her sing, no matter what it was—could be a spiritual, could be a corny show tune—he felt something. Her voice seemed to know things—there were secrets in it. Instead he just handed her a blues mix Caleb had burned for her and told her a little bit about the singers on it—Etta James, Ruth Brown, Koko Taylor. Just some secondhand tidbits and anecdotes he'd picked up from Caleb. But Nora was into it. She wanted to know more. She listened so intently—forehead scrunched in concentration, nodding as he talked, as if she were keeping the beat—it was a little unnerving. But he liked it. It made him feel interesting. Talking to Nora, he didn't feel adrift. He felt if only she'd listen to him long enough, he might figure out who he was.

"Not really," Fitz says.

"But there's someone. Maybe someone."

"Well sure, maybe," Fitz says. He feels himself starting to blush. "And your point?"

"My point is," his father says, "I wonder if this girl, this maybe girl, if she's ever made you foolish."

Nora is his maybe girl. Has she made him foolish? Not much. Not unless it's foolish to stare at the back of her head in biology class, to follow the ever-changing configurations of her amazing red hair, the complicated female business of holding it in place with an arsenal of bands, ties, and clips. Not unless it's foolish to study her picture in all his yearbooks, all the way back to elementary school, to follow her year-by-year transformation from gawky little girl into her current self. To memorize her schedule so that he can position himself at strategic locations throughout the school where she passes by. To imagine that they might someday study biology together, just the two of them. To hope. Is that foolish?

Because they have bottles in their hands, Fitz feels like there might be some kind of bar-room camaraderie between them, a couple of guys knocking a few back and talking about women. He almost says something about Nora. Almost. But stops himself.

Because he doesn't know this guy, not really. Maybe he was in the delivery room. So was the doctor. What does that prove? Anybody can hold a baby.

"I want to talk about you," Fitz says. He tries to put an edge back in his voice. "Your foolishness, not mine."

"Okay," his father says. "Sure."

"Did you guys, like, go out on dates? You and my mom?"

"Sure we did," his father says. "We went out on dates."

"You ask her out?"

"Yeah, I asked her out."

"What did you like about her?" Fitz asks. "Tell me about that. Curtis and Annie, sitting in a tree. That's the story I want to hear."

This is a test. As far as Fitz is concerned, it's pass-fail, make or break. A deal breaker. Does he even know her? Are they even talking about the same person?

14

"*Back then,*" his father tells Fitz, "she had an apartment on Grand Avenue. Right down the street from the place she worked. The diner. That's where we met—you know that, right? I was in law school, and that's where my buddy and I went to get something to eat after studying. She was our regular waitress."

Fitz shifts a little on the bench. He didn't know they met at a diner, but he's not about to let on. He shifts again—the gun is cutting into him. He wonders why all the movie gangsters hide weapons in their waistbands. It's super-uncomfortable. First chance he gets, Fitz decides, he's going to put it back in the pouch of his sweatshirt.

His father has paused and is watching him. "I'm listening," Fitz says. "Go on. She was your regular waitress."

"She lived in a basement apartment, with pipes and radiators on the ceiling. Except she hung strings of Christmas lights from the pipes, decorated with all kinds of colorful stuff—flowers, I think, sparkly streamer things, crepe paper. In Annie's apartment, every day was a holiday.

"The first time I picked her up for a date it took her the longest time to come to the door. I thought maybe I had the wrong day, the wrong time. I knocked again and waited some more. Of course, I was nervous. Finally, she opened the door. It was obvious she'd been crying: her eyes were all red, and there were little rivers of mascara running down her cheeks. She had a tissue wadded in one hand and some kind of dangerous-looking tool in the other hand, a wire cutter. Uh-oh, I thought. I'm in trouble now.

"But it wasn't about me. Not at all. 'Come in,' she said.

"On a coffee table in the living room there was this tiny plastic portable television—right out of the 1970s, or maybe the '60s. Some kind of relic. A museum piece. There was a bent coat hanger coming out of the set, a makeshift antenna. The TV was surrounded by little cups full of beads and stones, coils of wire, pliers—she was making jewelry back then. So that explained the wire cutter.

"She was watching *Casablanca*. The old movie. You know it?"

Fitz isn't stupid. Of course he knows it. Play it again, Sam. Humphrey Bogart and Ingrid Bergman. It's on cable about every other night. "Yeah," Fitz says. "I've heard of it."

"So okay. But the thing is, she's not really *watching* the movie. This television has no picture. The tube or whatever must be shot. The screen is dark. She's *listening* to the movie, that's what she's doing. She sits down, sets her wire cutter on the table, leans forward. Doesn't say a word—just points to the television. I figure, what the heck. I take a seat next to her on her little couch, and we both sit there, staring at the broken television, listening to the sound track. Pretty stupid, right? Like watching the radio.

It makes no sense. Except after a while, I'm drawn into it, the story, the voices, without distraction, just the sound of these people talking to each other.

"Then all of a sudden these little orange sparks start flickering in the back of the television. First one, then more. 'Annie,' I say, and point. But she shushes me. But then there's more sparks. I start to smell something burning. 'Annie,' I say again. 'This is the best part,' she says. So okay, I shut up.

"In the movie, they're at the airport. Rick is saying goodbye to Ilsa. A classic scene. I must have seen it before but never really heard it, not like this. Ilsa asking, 'What about us?' The airplane propellers. Bogey being Bogey. Annie is crying again now, too. I'm starting to feel a little choked up myself.

"That's when the TV set combusts. Not just sparks now, I'm talking about a flame. The television is on fire. This at least gets Annie's attention. She leaps up and yanks the plug from the wall. I pick up the television—the thing is hot!—Annie opens the apartment door for me and leads me to the Dumpster behind the building, and I toss it in. How's that for a way to start a first date?"

His father takes a drink of his water. It's like he's waiting for applause, some kind of response. And Fitz has to admit it: this guy is good. It's a good story. Fitz could practically see the sparks flying out of the television. He can't help but wonder, though: is it just a little too perfect? Fitz wonders if his father has told it before, how many times.

"We're talking about my mom," Fitz says. "What you liked about her."

"Sure," his father says. "What did I like about her?" He looks at the label of his water bottle, as if maybe the answer is printed there. "Everything," he says. "All of it. Her crappy television and her year-round Christmas lights. Her tears, her big heart. Her little cups of beads and her wire cutter. Her fearlessness. The whole package. I never met anyone like her before."

15

The woman in his father's story, that girl, that Annie—Fitz knows her. It's his mom, spot-on. The black-and-white movie sap. Staying up late to watch *The Philadelphia Story* for the zillionth time, giving him an elbow if he dares make a smart remark. His mom, the dollar-store Martha Stewart, forever fixing and fiddling, rigging and rearranging, their whole house like some never-ending arts-and-crafts project. That's his mom, all right.

If this were the final exam answer on the subject of his mom, his father passes with flying colors. He's in the ninetieth percentile. But Fitz doesn't let on. "That's a nice story," he says. He makes his voice flat, almost bored.

"I'm glad you liked it," his father says.

Fitz sips his water. He wonders if maybe Nora likes old movies. He wonders if he invited her over to watch *Casablanca*, would that make him seem interesting? If the picture went out, would she keep listening?

But what he needs to be thinking about right now is what's

next. *What'll we do with ourselves?* That's something Daisy asks Gatsby. That's what Fitz has got to figure out. What's he going to do with his father now?

There are other things to do at the park: more animals to see in the zoo, the paddleboats on the lake, ducks to feed, all the rides in the amusement park. In the happy home movie in his head, there are scenes of Fitz and his father on the bumper cars, the two of them getting strapped into the roller coaster.

But now, Fitz is not so sure. Thrill rides? His father doesn't seem like the type. As far as Fitz can determine, his father is looking for a smooth ride through life—that's why he drives a luxury car. He's not looking to get jostled. He's not interested in free fall. He doesn't want to get his hair messed up.

To be honest, Fitz is not even sure he's the type himself. With his mom, the Tilt-A-Whirl, that's about as wild as the two of them ever got. When he came to the park with Caleb, his friend was obsessed, as he often was, with the danger of things. Everyday objects. How easy it is to choke on a corn dog. More people are killed annually by vending machines than by sharks, Caleb likes to remind Fitz. But Caleb believes the point is not to relax while swimming in the ocean: instead, he believes, you should fear vending machines—they're more dangerous than sharks. Now, thanks to Caleb, Fitz can't help but notice how irresponsible all the ride operators look, how fragile the machinery seems, the rattletrap sound of it all.

Besides, Fitz knows he's got only so much time. The clock is ticking. It's already late in the morning. His mom gets home from work at four o'clock. He needs to be home before then, delete the message from the attendance office and answer his mom's after-school text.

He needs to make a decision, announce a plan. Kneel down and draw a play in the dirt. It's up to him.

"I think we should get something to eat," Fitz says. "I'm hungry."

"Good idea," his father says.

"I wanna go to that diner," Fitz says. It's where they met. That much he knows. It's like the scene of the crime.

"Okay," his father says. It bothers Fitz a little that his father is agreeing to the plan, as if he's got a say. Fitz is afraid he's losing control.

"We can do that," his father says. "But you gotta do one thing for me. When we get there, you gotta leave the gun in the car. Promise me that. I'm not gonna flee."

"How do I know?"

"Trust me."

"Trust you."

"You've got my wallet and my phone," his father says. "You've got my car keys. What am I gonna do? Walk away? Don't you see? I'm all in. I'm in it for the duration. I'm not going anywhere."

Fitz isn't sure what to say.

"If I run away," his father says, "you can come back tomorrow and shoot me. You know where I live. You can come back and shoot me every day for the rest of my life."

He smiles, just a little bit. But Fitz doesn't feel as if he's being laughed at. It's as if his father is amused at himself, or maybe by the two of them, this pickle they're in, together.

67

16

It's a little before noon, and there's a mix of people in the place. Some well-dressed business types, coming in for lunch. Some younger people in T-shirts and jeans, college age, lingering over egg-stained plates. A bearded, professor-looking guy is reading a book at the counter. In a back room, there's a round table ringed with mostly older women who seem like members of some kind of club or fellowship.

Fitz has eaten in a diner-style restaurant at the mall. It was like a diner theme park. You could get fried bologna, which was one of his mom's specialties, one of Fitz's favorite sandwiches since he was a little kid. But at the mall restaurant you weren't supposed to take it seriously. It was a joke. It was ironic bologna. You were supposed to laugh at it, laugh at yourself eating it, with the same attitude you might wear white socks and slick back your hair for a fifties sock hop.

This place isn't like that, not at all. No retro cutesy stuff on the walls. No obnoxious oldies Muzak. There's a glass case full of pies. There's a Polaroid of a cat taped to the register. Fitz can see a couple of wiry cooks in the back dressed in white T-shirts and grubby aprons, one of them, the guy scraping the grill, with forearms full of old-fashioned tattoos—anchors and eagles and such. Nothing ironic about him.

A sign tells them to seat themselves, and they slip into a booth near the windows. Fitz can see a boy about his own age on the street outside, waiting for a bus. He keeps leaning into the street to see what's coming. He has the same backpack as Fitz. Fitz wonders what this kid's backstory is, why he's not in school. A dropout? Skipping? Going to seek out *his* dad, wherever he is? Not likely. But who knows? The world is full of mysteries, everybody's got a story.

"So here we are," his father says. He cranes his neck and looks around. Takes two menus from behind a napkin holder and slides one over to Fitz.

"Seems like an okay place," Fitz says.

"You've never been here?" His father seems surprised. "Annie loved this place. It's like she owned it. She *was* this place."

A waitress brings them water. She's young and pretty. She's got rust-colored hair and cool glasses, big hoopy earrings and a tiny diamond in her nose. She's light on her feet, bopping to some private rhythm.

"How are you today, gentlemen?" she asks.

Fitz totally understands how you could fall in love with someone like her. She seems so happy to see them. It's like she's been waiting for them.

She doesn't look a thing like his mom, but still, Fitz guesses that he and his father are probably both thinking the same thing.

It's like they've traveled back in time. It's like this girl—Maddie, her name tag says—is playing the role of his mom in some back-to-the-future movie.

"I'll give you a few minutes," she says, and leaves them to look over their menus.

"We used to come here just about every night," his father says. "Rory and I. At, like, ten, eleven o'clock at night, talking all about contracts and torts. We were regulars." He looks out the window. There's a bus at the stop now, but the boy with Fitz's backpack isn't climbing aboard.

"Of course, that was a long time ago," his father says.

"Like fifteen years?"

"Something like that," his father says. They're talking about something and not talking about it, all at the same time. This is where they met, Annie and Curtis, his mom and dad. This is where it all started. This is where he started.

"So," Fitz says. "Did you have some kind of super-slick pickup line?"

His father looks offended. "Annie? You think she'd fall for a line? You think she'd go for slick?"

Fitz almost says something but stops himself. This morning, Fitz was certain that his father was slick, or at the very least, slick in a past life, a guy formerly known as slick. Now he's not so sure. On the question of his father's slickness, he's currently agnostic. He decides to keep his mouth shut.

"Sometimes," his father says, "when it was slow, she'd go back into the kitchen and fix our food herself. She'd make us these grilled sandwiches that weren't even on the menu.

70

"Then we'd talk," his father says. "She'd finish her side work and pull up a chair. The place was dead. That's how we got to know each other. The old-fashioned way. Nothing slick about it. What you guys do online, we did in person. Very old-school."

"About what?" Fitz asks. He doesn't want to hear about you-kids-and-your-technology. "What did you talk about?"

"Movies," his father says. "Books. Anything and everything. The meaning of life. How much I hated law school. We talked about that a lot."

Now Maddie the waitress comes back to their booth. "What can I get you guys?" she asks.

There's a lot of stuff on the menu—melts and combinations, specials like walleye and bratwurst—but Fitz has zeroed in on something. He says he'll have a deluxe burger, medium—bacon, American cheese, mayo, and sautéed onions.

"Oh yeah," Maddie says. She nods and smiles, as if to say, of course, what else would a cool person order? It's stupid, but Fitz is grateful for her approval.

His father closes his menu with a kind of emphatic slap. "The same," he says.

"All right," Maddie says, "you got it," and off she goes.

"She was a wonder," his father says. "Never wrote anything down either. She remembered how you liked your eggs, what kind of toast, wheat or rye, dark or light, the whole bit, what you wanted on the side. She cut tremendous pieces of pie, gave you epic scoops of ice cream. It made her happy to feed people."

Once again, Fitz feels sort of unsettled and impressed. His father knows his mom, that's for sure.

She is always happy as can be in the kitchen, making a big weekend breakfast, just like a short-order cook. Frying a pan of bacon and putting it aside. Then making eggs, scrambled for Fitz, over easy for his grandpa when he was alive, with onions and green peppers for Uncle Dunc. French toast for Caleb, whose mom doesn't cook, who barely microwaves. Omelets, pancakes, hash browns, whatever you want, she puts it together, talking the whole time, working two or three burners, a total pro.

Fitz has always loved the cheerful, professional way his mom puts a plate of food in front of him, with a kind of stylish pride.

"So has it changed?" Fitz asks. "Since then?"

His father looks around. "Not much. Same menu, same booths. Really, not a bit. Just me.

"I feel like what's-his-name," his father says. "In *A Christmas Carol*. Visiting scenes of his happy youth."

"Scrooge," Fitz says. "Ebenezer Scrooge. That's his name." It sounds like an accusation. Which it is.

"Right," his father says. He says it softly, reluctantly even. "Scrooge." When he says it, it sounds like a confession.

Fitz knows the story. He's seen all the different movie versions. His mom's favorite, naturally, is the old black-and-white one, Alastair Somebody-or-Other shivering in his nightshirt. If it's on, she's got to watch it. Fitz likes Bill Murray. That's his favorite Scrooge.

"Then who am I?" Fitz asks. "If you're Scrooge? Tiny Tim?"

"Oh no," his father says. "Not Tiny Tim. No way."

He takes a sip of water. "You're the ghost," his father says. "My ghost. That's who you are. That's exactly who you are."

17

Fitz and his father both have their mouths full of deluxe burger when all of a sudden there's a man at their booth, a guy looming over them in a black suit.

"Curtis?" the man says. "Curtis Powell?"

Dude looks like serious law enforcement—white shirt, close-cropped hair, a gizmo in his ear—FBI or Homeland Security or something. In an instant, Fitz can envision a chain of shame and humiliation—handcuffs, mug shots, a holding cell, a call to his mom. So this is how it ends.

But first his father needs to finish chewing and swallow. They've both just taken huge juicy bites. His father raises his hand, like he's asking for time. Fitz sees a grease spot on his tie the size of a dime.

It occurs to Fitz that if this guy hauls him away, he's never going to finish his lunch. Somehow, this seems worse than any dire legal consequences. Him downtown, and his burger, more than half of it, pretty much the best burger he's ever had, and his fries, sitting on a plate in an empty booth, getting cold, getting taken away by Maddie and then tossed. It feels tragic. To go through life with this burger unfinished. How could you not feel off balance and incomplete forever afterward?

Finally, his father swallows. "Chip," he says. He wipes his hand quickly on a paper napkin and extends it to the man.

"Curtis," the man says. "I knew it was you. You still downtown? Still with Daugherty?"

This guy is no cop. A Bluetooth, that's what he's got in his ear. Just a telephone.

"Still with Daugherty," his father says.

"Working downtown but coming here to the diner for lunch," this Chip says. "Classic. That's what it is. I love it." He glances at Fitz.

"Let me introduce you," his father says. "Chip Slocum, this is Fitzgerald."

Fitz has wiped his chin and his hands. He's ready. "Pleased to meet you." He thinks he likes it that his father has gone with just the one name, like Madonna and Prince, Bono and Flea—Fitzgerald, the one and only. It makes him feels like somebody.

He feels at a disadvantage, though, sitting down, talking up, but there's no way to squeeze out. Turns out it doesn't really matter. Chip is not especially interested in him. Fitz thinks he might wonder what occasion would bring two such unlikely companions together—Take an Urchin to Work Day?—but the man seems to show no curiosity whatsoever.

"And you?" his father asks. "Still at Cooke?"

"Yup, yup," Chip says.

"Business good?" his father asks. "Life good?"

"All good," Chip says. "No call for your expertise. Thank goodness. No offense."

"None taken. I'm happy to hear it."

"No more issues on that front," Chip says. "Knock on wood." He makes a show of rapping on the wood-looking edge of their table.

His father touches his own fist to the laminate in solidarity. "That's great," he says.

Fitz notices that his father's demeanor is different now from what it's been with him. He seems stiffer somehow, more brittle, but also less substantial, less present. It's like he can see him fading around the edges. Like a hologram. He doesn't like it.

"Well, listen," Chip says. "I'll let you get back to your lunch. Say hello for me to your colleague. The tall fellow. And your nice assistant."

"Jerry," his father says. "And Sheila. Will do. Absolutely."

Chip departs then, strolling toward the back of the restaurant, his head swiveling, looking to see who else he might know.

"You his lawyer?" Fitz asks. He picks up his burger and takes a bite, a modest one.

"I did some work for him," his father says. "We represent his company."

"What did he do?" Somehow Fitz can easily imagine this guy needing to get all lawyered up, guilty of something somehow, doing a perp walk for some corporate crime. "What was the issue?"

"Wrongful termination," his father says.

"He killed somebody?"

His father laughs, emits a series of soft little syllables of amusement, for the first time today. It makes Fitz feel good, proud even, that he can make him laugh. He's funny, he wants his father to know that about him. It's one of his best qualities. He cracks up his mom a couple of times a day.

"Fired somebody," he says. "That's what he did."

"You get him off?" Fitz asks.

"It's not like that," his father says. "It's civil, not criminal. And it wasn't him personally who got sued, it was his company. The corporation."

"So did you get them off, the corporation?"

"We settled."

"Paid 'em off."

"Something like that."

"He seems like a jerk," Fitz says. There was something about the guy that just wasn't trustworthy. For one thing, Chip doesn't seem like a serious name for an adult. Plus, Fitz hates middle-aged guys with earpieces. Plus, the idea of a settlement burns him. It's a little too close to home.

You can treat someone badly, then give them money, how is that okay?

"What if they're guilty?" Fitz asks. "The corporations you represent? What if they're evil? What if they're, like, terrible polluters? What if the company is spewing poison into the air, cutting down the rain forests? Or what if they discriminate? What if they treat their workers like crap? What then?"

"If you get sued, you have the right to tell your side of the story. There are two sides to every story. You know that."

There are two sides to every story, Fitz's grandpa used to tell him. And then there's the truth.

"I help them tell their story," his father says. "It's how the system operates. Somebody's got to do it."

Fitz gets that. He's not naive. He understands the system. But still. It's disappointing. There's a lot of stuff that's got to be done. But you don't have to be the one who does it. Fitz thinks of one of his mom's favorite expressions, what she tells him when he tries to get away with something—using SparkNotes, say—because other kids do it. *You're better than that.* That's what she tells him.

"He *is* a jerk," his father says. "You got that right."

Fitz looks over his shoulder and sees the back of the Chipster's bullet head a few tables away, talking in the direction of a couple of guys who already look bored and tired of him.

"Maybe, if we're lucky," Fitz says, "he'll stay away. Maybe we won't have any more issues on that front." He raps the tabletop with his right hand, and for the second time his father laughs.

18

They both order apple pie for dessert. Maddie brings it to them warm, with ice cream. The pieces are huge, tall slices of apple layered in some geologic way, crumbly stuff on top. Cinnamon, apples, brown sugar, vanilla—it may be Fitz's favorite smell in the world. He leans over it and inhales. If this were a drug, he'd be a junkie.

His mom bakes pies just for special occasions—Thanksgiving, Uncle Dunc's birthday—sometimes blueberry, but usually apple, always with little pictures or messages etched into the top crust: a turkey, a heart, a smiley face.

Fitz thanks Maddie, picks up his fork, and digs in. He finishes his pie in less than a minute. When he's done, he feels a little out of breath. But he can't help himself. It is awesome apple pie.

When Maddie swings by their table to see how they're doing, how they're liking it, Fitz is embarrassed. His mom is always on him to slow down. He knows it's rude to bolt down your food.

She looks at the apple and ice cream smear on his plate. "You know what you need?" she asks.

Fitz is afraid that she's going to say something like "better manners." It will kill him if she shames him.

Maddie puts a hand on her hip and turns toward his father. His piece of pie is still more or less intact, just a couple of neat forkfuls removed from the edges. "You know what he needs, don't you?"

"I know."

She points at Fitz, a kind of Uncle Sam gesture, only infinitely cuter. "You need another piece of pie." She consults his father again. "Am I right?" she asks. "Or am I right?"

"You are so right," his father says. "Right as rain."

"Because he's a growing boy," she says. "And he's starving."

"We need to do something," his father says.

"More pie," Maddie says. "That's what the boy needs."

All of a sudden, they're double-teaming him. They've formed some kind of alliance, reached an understanding, and the basis of it, the core principle, is that he, Fitz, needs more of what he loves. He feels himself blushing. He's not really used to being the center of attention, not like this.

A second piece of pie, in a restaurant—it just never even occurred to Fitz as a possibility. It violates some iron law, some rule so fundamental and obvious and universally accepted that it never needs to be spelled out: *each diner may order one, and only one, dessert.* But today that rule doesn't apply. Today, all bets are off.

In just a couple of minutes, Maddie is back with another piece of pie, more ice cream. "Okay, champ," she says. "Dig in."

Fitz looks at his father. "You heard her," his father says.

It seems to Fitz now, at this moment, with his father and a pretty girl smiling at him, a gorgeous piece of apple pie in front of him, that no matter what happens to him afterward, even if he is arrested, cuffed, expelled, no matter what punishment he suffers for his crazy stunt today, no matter what, it will have been worth it.

His father has his fork in hand. He's doing some excavating and rearranging on his plate, but mainly he's watching Fitz. It looks like he's enjoying Fitz's enjoyment, feeling his pie pleasure once removed.

Before he starts in on his pie, he wants to tell his father something. "Fitz," he says. "That's what they call me."

19

Fitz reaches across the table and picks up the check that Maddie left in front of his father. He calculates what would be a generous tip and pulls his father's wallet from his hip pocket.

He almost feels as if he should keep it hidden from his father. It's wrong that he has it. Fitz knows that. It's a reminder, pie or no pie, of how things stand between them.

A wallet is personal, intimate even, and Fitz tries to respect that. There's some credit cards in there, maybe some photographs, who knows what else, but he doesn't look. He extracts a few bills as dispassionately as he can. For his part, his father doesn't betray any emotion. He doesn't look pained or outraged or violated in any way. His expression is completely neutral. Fitz wonders how you do that, imagines it must be a lawyer thing.

Fitz drops the bills on the table. It feels good. To have the dough. To know there's more where that came from. It's not like when he and Caleb go out for French fries and Dr Peppers with their pockets full of change, worrying that the sales tax is going to bust them.

Maybe this is what it feels like to be Dad. The man with the wallet. At the same time, he's worrying about where he's taking this show next. He's feeling the weight of being in charge. Maybe that's part of the dad equation, too. He's picking up the tabs and calling the shots. He's the man. He can see how you might love it, and also how you might get tired of it.

He thinks about asking his father, *is that what it feels like?* But really, how would he know? He's the wrong guy to ask.

20

Fitz excuses himself and hits the restroom. The men's is down a long hallway in the far back of the restaurant, marked by a Ken doll stuck on the door, which Fitz thinks is a nice touch. Ken is shirtless, displaying impressive plastic pecs, sporting plaid shorts and sandals.

While he's washing his hands, Fitz imagines that they might become regulars here, he and his father. Maddie would remember him, the apple pie boy. They might strike up a little friendship. Why not? He looks in the mirror and fluffs his hair a little. Anything is possible.

When Fitz comes back out, their booth is empty. There's a guy in an apron loading their dishes into a big plastic tub. He can see the ravaged, smashed remnants of his father's pie. His father is nowhere to be seen.

Fitz feels a flutter of panic in his gut. All his stuff is in the car. The gun is in the car. He has his father's wallet and phone but he let him keep his car keys. How could he be so stupid?

He scans the place—people are eating, studying their menus,

Chip is gesturing at someone in a semi-threatening way with a fork. Fitz moves quickly between the booths, stifling his urge to run, keeping himself in check. His father's not at the front of the restaurant near the register. He's not in the foyer.

Fitz steps outside and looks up and down the block. The kid with his backpack is still standing there at the bus stop. He gives Fitz a look: *Do I know you? Am I supposed to know you?*

Fitz goes back inside. He returns to their booth, which is clean and set up now, shiny and empty, as if they've never been there, as if the lunch never happened. He feels like the sole victim in some scam or prank everyone else is in on. He feels like he's wandered into *The Twilight Zone*.

Just then Maddie the waitress comes by with a tray full of water glasses. She smiles, looking genuinely happy to see him, which is a little gift he's too upset to appreciate right now. Then she seems to take in his distress. Her face gets serious. "You forget something?"

"I'm looking," he says. "I'm looking for *him*. Did you see him leave?"

"Your dad," she says, and he doesn't contradict her. She makes a kind of thinking face. Then she brightens. "He's on the phone," she says. "Thataway."

"Thanks," Fitz says. "Thanks a lot."

"Just doin' my job," he hears her say as he turns in the direction of the back of the restaurant.

Sure enough. He's standing there, hunched, turned away, a telephone receiver held tight to his ear. Fitz must have walked right by him on his way out of the men's room. The last pay phone in America, and he's found it.

His father sees Fitz then. He holds the receiver away from his ear and rolls his eyes a little. He doesn't look especially busted, not at all apologetic.

"I thought we had a deal," Fitz says. He hears his voice catch a little. He's in the throes of some weird new emotion, some blend of betrayal and relief. It must be how a parent feels when a lost child has been found. You wanna hug 'em, and you wanna smack 'em.

"Just checking my messages," he says.

"Right," Fitz says. Now he's feeling it again, something simpler, what he felt back at the park, the slow boil. "And now you're done checking your messages. It's time to go."

21

"Just drive," Fitz told his father when they got in the car outside the diner, and that's what he's doing. They're on the River Road now, the Minneapolis side, following the curves of the Mississippi, seeing the joggers and walkers and bikers on the path.

Fitz is thinking about what his father told him. So far, the dots are still not connecting. The story is not quite tracking. This is what he knows: They met at a diner. She made awesome sandwiches. They talked. He picked her up for a date. Her television blew up. He met her father and they did not hit it off. Fitz was born, and his father held him long enough for a picture to be taken. He went to St. Louis. Fifteen and a half years passed, and here they are. You could say there are a few holes in the story.

"So why'd you come back?" Fitz asks. This is what lawyers do, they ask questions. They interrogate, they cross-examine. The good ones are relentless. They scare people. You see it in all the courtroom dramas. They go after lies, contradictions, weakness, soft spots. Maybe, Fitz thinks, he can give his father a dose of his own medicine.

"Come back?"

"To St. Paul. Why?" Fitz knows that Gatsby did not end up across the bay from Daisy by accident. It was part of a plan.

"It was a good job."

"You had a good job, right? There are good jobs all over the country."

"This was a perfect fit."

"It just happened to be here. Is that what you're saying? It's a coincidence. Same job, in Omaha? You take it?"

"Nothing wrong with Omaha," his father says.

Fitz so wants to believe that his father came back to St. Paul to be near him. He wants to hear him say it. He's tried—what do they call it?—leading the witness, but it's no good. He's going to have to try another line of questioning.

There's a lot more that he's curious about. Like, how did his mom even get pregnant? Didn't they have sex education back then? Nobody took Health? He's too embarrassed to ask. He doesn't want to go there. But you'd think they would have known better.

They slow down on a curve and Fitz gets a good view of a happy little family on the walking path: Mom pushing a stroller, Dad with a yellow lab on a leash. It's a weekday afternoon, but there they are, strolling in the sunshine. They could be in a public service announcement for family togetherness.

"So what happened?" Fitz says. "What went wrong?"

"What do you mean?" his father asks.

"Something went wrong. You broke up with Mom," Fitz says. "You broke up with me."

Of course, that's the issue. Not that his parents aren't together. In his catalog of fathers, there are plenty of divorced dads, several varieties, Caleb's, for instance. He's got a stepdad now—that's a whole separate species—but his dad-dad, he checks in at Christmas and birthdays with gifts for Caleb and his sister. He takes them up north for a week in the summer. When Caleb screws up, gets a bad grade, his dad calls and gives him a talking-to. It's not perfect—Caleb rolls his eyes about his father's terrible taste in music, he's not fond of his new girlfriend—but the man is on the job, he's in the mix.

"It wasn't about you," his father says. "It was never about you."

Fitz feels another quick, hot surge of anger. Your father bails on you, takes a fifteen-year hike, and then says it's not about you. It's a good thing probably that the gun is zipped into his backpack. In movies, when someone says something so stupid to a real tough guy, he gets pistol-whipped. Fitz totally understands the temptation.

They're on a bridge now, crossing over from Minneapolis back into St. Paul. Below, the Mississippi is shimmering in the afternoon sun.

"What was it about, then?" Fitz says. He's looking out the window, staring down at the river. There's something almost hypnotic about it, it's calming him down to watch it. "Tell me that."

"We were so different," his father says. "From different worlds, that's what she used to say."

That sounds like another soap opera to Fitz, maybe a romance novel. Now Fitz is feeling not so much angry as exhausted. Maybe it's his belly full of burger and apple pie. Maybe his father's line of bull is making him sleepy. He feels almost too tired to call him out.

They're exiting the bridge now, and Fitz turns to get a last look at the river. He remembers seeing the source, on vacation in northern Minnesota with his mom, and there, at the headwaters, in Itasca Park, he and his mom waded across in a few quick steps. It made an impression. Something so modest, a shallow trickle, could become swift and powerful, dangerous even, a force to be reckoned with.

It's the same river that flows through St. Louis, where Chuck Berry grew up, where his father lived, all the way down to the Delta, home to the bluesmen that Caleb so reveres and refers to sometimes by first name, as if they are still alive, as if he knows them, as if they are kids from school. "This is how Robert would play it," Caleb might say, and Fitz knows he's talking about Robert Johnson, who died in something like 1930. On the other end of this same river is New Orleans, Fats Domino, the Ninth Ward, all those people stranded on roofs and stuck in the Superdome. His mom watched them on television, tears streaming down her face. Somehow they are all connected by it, this river, Fitz and his father and his mom and the folks down there. Fitz wishes he could find a way to write a song about that.

22

Fitz flips up the hood of his sweatshirt. It is a kind of private signal with his mom, half joke and half not, his own personal do-not-disturb sign. It's what he does when he doesn't feel like talking, when he needs a little Fitz time. It's how he retracts into his shell when he feels vulnerable. He's read somewhere that some rock star, Dylan probably, somebody legendary, communicates this way with his people—when the hood is up, it means *I don't wanna talk*. It means *leave me alone*. Fitz loves the wordless efficiency of the gesture—no need to explain, which is exactly the point—and he sometimes likes the sensation of being insulated from the world. It's a way for him to step back. It's not as if all his clothing is hooded—though a surprisingly large percentage of his wardrobe does indeed consist of hoodies—and it's not all that often, really, that he feels the need. But sometimes he does. Especially in the car, he's glad to have a no-chat option with his mom, who may smile a little when he flips up but always respects his preference. It works for him, with his mom at least.

His father obviously doesn't know the code, doesn't speak the language. Right now he seems to be in his own world, too. He might as well be hooded. He's off in his own place, wherever that it is.

Fitz unzips the front pocket of his backpack and takes out a CD. It's got a handful of songs they recorded the week before, just Fitz and Caleb and a drum machine, a few covers and one original. It isn't a demo or anything, just something to show for all their time in Caleb's basement. Fitz isn't sure why he packed it this morning. He wasn't really planning on playing it. But right now it feels like the right thing to do. They're in the middle of something, going from one thing to the next, scenery whizzing by them—it's the perfect time for, what do they call it? A musical interlude.

The first song on it is them doing a number by Jimmy Reed, one of Caleb's heroes. He wasn't blind, but he did have epilepsy and was an alcoholic, too, of course. A couple of weeks before, Caleb gave Fitz a CD of his songs. Told Fitz he should try to write something like it, but there was no way. If you copied out the lyrics to one of his songs, they didn't look like much.

> *Ain't that lovin' you, baby?*
> *Ain't that lovin' you, baby?*
> *Ain't that lovin' you, baby?*
> *But you don't even know my name.*

They didn't always even seem to make a lot of sense. It was like the song might have been made out of phrases written on scraps of paper and pulled out of a hat or something. But somehow still, the songs got under Fitz's skin.

Probably it was Jimmy's vocals, the knowing, lazy way he sang, that made Fitz feel something that wasn't on the page. It was all about wanting, wanting something you didn't have, wanting it with every ounce of your being. It was like Jimmy knew all about having a hole at the center of yourself. The songs had some kind of New Orleans beat—it was happy music, it made you want to move your feet—but underneath it all, there was something else, something desperate and incurable.

Fitz slips in the disc and hits play. The song they cover is "I Wanna Be Loved." Strumming his guitar's bottom strings with a thumb pick, Caleb sounds a little like Jimmy. He has recently acquired a harmonica rack, which he is awfully proud of, and manages to play some decent harp fills. Fitz is playing a boogie-woogie shuffle on the bass. Caleb's singing is passable. He sounds a little less weary than Jimmy, he sounds more urgent, he's got a little punk edge, but it works all right.

> I wanna be loved but by only you
> Because I know, I know your love is true.

Fitz turns it up a little, adjusts the balance. They sound pretty good on his father's fancy sound system, just not enough bass, which Fitz corrects. He wishes Caleb could hear for himself.

His father cocks his head to show that he's listening. Fitz wants him to like it. To be impressed even. Wowed. And he hates himself for caring. Why should it even matter what this guy thinks of him? What does he know about music? Fitz shouldn't give a damn one way or another. He shouldn't crave his approval. But he does.

"That's you, right?" his father says. "Your band?"

"Yeah," Fitz says.

His father listens some more. "I like your sound," he says. "You have a nice groove going. I don't think many kids your age understand the blues. But you guys got it, you really got it."

He is saying all the right things. But Fitz doesn't trust it. He doesn't trust him. Everything he says could mean just what it says. Or it could mean something else entirely. "I like your sound" could mean "I like your sound." Or it could mean "Maybe you ought to consider taking some lessons." It could mean "All right, I listened, you satisfied?" Or it could even mean "Please don't shoot me."

Fitz could try to figure it out. He could try to turn himself into a human lie detector. Study his father's breathing and gestures, try to tune in to his micro-expressions, practice the same kind of close reading Mr. Massey makes them perform on poems—weigh every syllable, measure connotation, tone, implication, understatement. But it's exhausting. Plus he's not very good at it. He's had so little practice. When Caleb says something like "Dude, there's something wrong with your hair, it looks *frightened*," there's not much doubt about what he's getting at. When his mom looks at his report card, even the less-than-stellar marks in French, and tells him, "I'm proud of you," it never occurs to Fitz that she might mean something other than just that.

Fitz hears himself stumble just a second on the song's last turn-around and peeks at his dad to gauge his reaction. He feels a warm flush of shame. He leans forward and hits the stop button.

23

They're on Summit Avenue now. It's St. Paul's postcard street: lined with trees, a grassy median down the middle, wide sidewalks, and on both sides churches and mansions, mansions and churches. It's like they're inside a coffee table book. Fitz thinks these streets, these cities, must have some kind of hold on his father. They must exert some gravitational pull on him. He went to law school here, but then he moved to St. Louis. That's where the checks came from. He must have had a nice place to live, he must have had friends there, some places there where he played tennis and bought fancy coffee and shopped for produce. But he came back. Fitz doesn't quite buy the good-job line. And now, just driving around, this is where he directs the car.

Somewhere on this street is where F. Scott Fitzgerald lived when he was a kid. His namesake. His mom's favorite.

Fitz wonders what she's doing now. She's had her lunch already and has been outside on the playground with the little kids, pushing them on the swings. No idea that he's rolling around town with his father. Probably she's working with Wesley, a new boy with such a terrible history she's only hinted at it.

All the kids at her school have issues, problems, every one of them a bundle of deficits and special needs. That's what the school is all about. But her favorite kids, her special projects, the ones she talks about at dinner, are always the most damaged and beaten up, the toughest cases, the ones who've lost the most. Kids like Wesley.

Even though they've never met, Fitz feels like he knows Wesley. His mom talks about him all the time. He's like a character in a book they're reading together, day by day, chapter by chapter. "Wesley Makes Friends with Snickers the Hamster." "Wesley and the 500-Piece Jigsaw Puzzle."

But he's real, Fitz knows that, with real problems. Wesley is just a little younger than Fitz, thirteen maybe, but has been in foster care since his father sold him for drug money, his mom told Fitz that much. Now he rarely speaks, never makes eye contact, and sometimes, for no apparent reason, flies off into a rage.

His mom said she thought Wesley liked *Star Wars*, so Fitz gave her some of his old action figures—Chewbacca, Luke, Boba Fett, a couple of droids—to bring in for him. She said he liked them. So he imagines his mom playing *Star Wars* with this boy, Wesley, the same way she played with him when he was little, moving them across a tabletop, making up a story together.

"You grow up here?" Fitz asks. "In St. Paul?"

"Here?" his father says. "No."

"Where?"

"Chicago," he says, but then corrects himself. "A suburb." Fitz can imagine it. A rich kid. There was a big green lawn, tennis lessons. It makes perfect sense.

"Your dad was a lawyer, too, right?"

His father looks surprised. "How'd you know?"

"Lucky guess." It isn't rocket science. The guy hated law school. So why would you even go in the first place? "Your parents," Fitz says. "My grandparents?"

His father's face changes. It gets stony. "What about them?"

"Where are they?"

"My dad passed away. My mom lives in Florida."

"Brothers and sisters?"

"One sister. A neurologist. In Boston. Married to another neurologist."

"And how about you? You ever married?"

"No."

"Why not?"

"It's complicated."

"Sure," Fitz says. He looks out the window. Everything's complicated. How do you sell a kid? That's gotta be complicated, too. Why did he think this guy would give him a straight answer? He's a lawyer. He's all about complication.

They're stopped at a red light.

"We thought about it," his father says. "Your mom and me."

Fitz tries to imagine the two of them getting married, coming down the steps of one of these Summit Avenue churches, people throwing rice, or birdseed, or whatever it is that people throw. Curtis in a tuxedo, Fitz can totally see that, rocking a black tie and cummerbund. Tails probably. He'd cut a dashing figure. His mom in a wedding dress, all frilled and lacy, not so much. Not at all, really.

"But you didn't," Fitz says.

"No," his father says. "But I wanted to."

"Just because," Fitz says.

"Not just because. Because I thought she was the one. Even before you, I thought that."

So what happened? Fitz wonders. This is what he needs to know. This is why he bought a gun. If he has to wave it in his face some more to get him to answer, so be it.

What happened? He's in the delivery room. He's giving her books. He's thinking she's the one. And then he's gone. Out of the picture. Mailing it in from Missouri. Something happened.

24

"*I have to ask you a favor,*" his father says.

The possibility that he might be able to do something for his father, to give him something—that interests Fitz. It makes him feel important. "Really," he says. Whatever it is, he's inclined to say yes. He can show his father that he's not only funny and a decent bass player but that he's generous, too.

His father explains that he needs to go into his office and sign something—a motion. If it's not filed with the clerk by five o'clock, he's in trouble. Fitz feels a kind of embarrassed sinking. He's been hoping for something personal, some kind of intimacy. *Tell me*, something along those lines. *Forgive me.* Some special favor only he can confer. Instead, his father is asking for what—work release?

"How much trouble?" Fitz wants to know.

"Big trouble," his father says. "A boatload. If I miss this deadline, we go to trial unprepared. I could get sued. Slapped with malpractice."

"Could you get fired?" Fitz asks.

"Maybe."

It's an appealing thought. Imagining his father being brought down. Fitz feels a certain pleasure in contemplating that. Some big boss man chewing him out. Telling him to clear out, clean out his desk.

But really, Fitz wonders, how could that be? It doesn't sound right. So much riding on one guy's signature. Who's that important?

They're coming into downtown St. Paul now, the capitol dome behind them, passing the science museum he used to visit with his mom, aiming straight for his father's building. Fitz realizes that they've been headed to his office all along, even before he asked. It bothers Fitz that even today, his father can't put away his work. That he has to share him. "They can't get along without you? For one lousy day?"

"It'll only take five minutes," his father says. "I give it a quick read-through and sign my name."

"What if you were sick?" Fitz asks. "I mean, really sick?"

"I'd come in, sign, and go back to bed."

"What if you were in the hospital? What if you were hooked up to an IV? What if you were on life support? What if you slipped into a coma? What then? You're telling me one of your lawyer buddies couldn't sign?"

"Five minutes."

"What about me?" Fitz asks. "You crack a window and leave me in the car like a dog?"

"No," his father tells him. "No, no, no. Of course not. You

come along with me. I can show you around. After that, I'm all yours."

"Sure," Fitz says. "Five minutes." His father's face brightens. He looks as happy as he has all day. Fitz really has done him a favor. It's just not the one he wanted.

25

The firm of Plunkett and Daugherty takes up the entire twelfth floor of its building. They enter through two heavy, carved wooden doors, church doors. In the reception area, there are plants, muted abstract oil paintings on the wall, leather chairs, architectural magazines fanned out on a coffee table.

Here, Fitz feels dirty and disreputable, unkempt and unwashed. With his backpack slung over his shoulder, he feels homeless, a guy toting his belongings with him wherever he goes. In the car, back in the parking ramp, his father straightened his tie and fixed his hair in the rearview mirror. He put on his suit jacket, and now, fully wardrobed in his lawyer getup, he seems completely at ease.

The receptionist is a young woman in a black blouse wearing a headset, her hair pulled back austerely in a bunnish configuration. "Hello, Mr. Powell," she says. She pushes a button in front of her. "Plunkett and Daugherty," she says. "How may I direct your call?"

Fitz's father gives her a little wave and motions to the left, this way. Fitz follows him down a long hallway, past offices, some with their doors open. He catches a glimpse of a silver-haired man in a bow tie and suspenders talking on the phone—he looks like the popcorn guy. They pass a kitchenette smelling of garlic, a little like his mom's homemade red sauce.

His father pauses then and opens a door on the left. This is his office, his natural habitat, his lawyer lair. It's more modest than Fitz imagined. He's been picturing his father seated in some kind of padded, spinning leather throne, his desk ornate and expansive, the kind of place where sinister moguls in movies devise their evil plans. In fact, the office is neat—tasteful and understated.

There are framed diplomas on the wall and a painting of a sailboat. On the desk, there's a computer monitor, a calendar, a leather cup full of pens. There's a tall bookcase full of legal volumes, a credenza with a neat stack of file folders on it. No souvenirs, no knickknacks. No photographs. Nothing that implicates him in the life of another human being.

Fitz's father stands at his desk and pushes a couple of buttons on his phone. He picks up a pen and makes a note on his calendar. His face takes on that half-abstracted, mildly impatient look people get when they listen to a recorded message.

His mom's space at her school—it's not quite an office, a kind of cubby really, just a desk and bulletin board in the back of a classroom—is full of personal stuff, most of it Fitz-related: primitive animal drawings he made back in elementary school; a full set of his school photos, before and after braces, his hair changing gradually, growing out from a buzz cut to its current style, Sgt. Pepper–era Beatles; a flyer for a coffeehouse gig that Fitz and Caleb were going to play except the place closed down first. It's almost embarrassing. Like a museum exhibit: Fitz Through the Ages. But really, if it all disappeared somehow, if he ever came in and discovered that she'd remodeled and upgraded, replaced his ragged art with some framed sailboats, it would be upsetting, more than upsetting, it would be *wrong*.

Fitz wonders if his father's apartment looks like this on the inside. Generically neat and professional, like something from one of those magazines in the lobby. Not like the mess that's always fermenting at his house. The dining room table full of Fitz's schoolbooks—Homework Central, his mom calls it—alongside her latest school project—construction paper and stencils, glue and glitter. The kitchen counter piled high with secondhand books from the latest library sale. The fridge entirely covered with magneted stuff, a crazy paper tree in full bloom: report cards, school notices, a snapshot of Uncle Dunc with a monster muskie he landed years ago, pictures from newspapers and magazines Fitz and his mom have cut out and posted over the years for no apparent reason—B.B. King, Kaiser Wilhelm, Toni Morrison.

A woman comes into the room. "There you are," she says. She's aiming for his father but pauses when she notices Fitz, who is just sort of standing there, lurking.

"My name is Sheila," she says. She says this toward Fitz, in his general direction. He recognizes her name. It's the woman that Chip at the diner wanted his father to greet. She's older than Fitz expects an assistant to be, not old-old but older than his father. She looks like a fifth-grade teacher, a nice one.

Fitz expects his father to come in at this point, but there's an awkward pause. For a moment, Fitz thinks his father is going to deny any knowledge of him, act like Fitz just followed him into the office, a stray. But then he speaks up. "And this," he says, pausing just a beat, "is Fitz."

In his father's mouth, his name sounds good. He hasn't always loved his name—he downright hates being Fitzgerald on all the official class rosters—but even corrected, reduced to a single memorable syllable, it sometimes seems too odd. He is always the only one. But now, when his father says it, it has a certain dignity. Right now, it makes him glad, even proud, to be Fitz.

"Pleased to meet you," she says. She smiles. She looks genuinely pleased. If she is repulsed or frightened by his grubby self, she doesn't show it.

She turns to his father then. "This has all the changes," she says, and hands a sheaf of papers to him.

His father stands there reading, turning the long legal sheets, making little sounds of approval, Sheila watching him read. There are little arrowed transparent thingies sticking out between the pages, marking the spots, Fitz supposes, where he's supposed to sign.

Fitz walks over to the window. It's an amazing view. He can see people on the sidewalks below. From this distance, they look like miniatures, like toys—cute little people going about their little lives. He remembers a story Caleb told him once about a friend of his who worked as a salad boy at a downtown hotel and used to go up on the roof late at night and throw vegetables at pedestrians—two, three blocks away, some guy would get nailed with a cherry tomato and have no idea where it came from. Now, standing here and looking down at the world, Fitz can maybe understand the urge. If he had an open window and some veggies at hand, no telling what he might do.

Two blocks away he can see the top of a metro bus making a wide turn. It's one of the new green buses, just like the one he boarded this morning. It's hard for Fitz to believe that it was only hours ago. It seems like that was another year, another lifetime. In a space between two other buildings, he can see the Mississippi again. It's the third or fourth time he's seen it today. Every time, it looks different. It changes color, like a mood ring. Now the sky is getting overcast, and the water looks gray.

Across the river is his house, his neighborhood, his life. Somewhere over there, his mom is working. Caleb is at school, in sixth-period study hall now, a little annoyed with Fitz probably for his no-show.

He can almost imagine himself there, too. Across the river. Going about his business. Some other version of himself, not his gun-toting, outlaw self—his everyday self, his law-abiding, rule-respecting, good-kid, low-maintenance self. Yesterday, that kid was sitting at a desk, doing his homework, following directions. And tomorrow? Is he going to step back into that life as if nothing happened? It doesn't seem possible.

"Okay," his father says. "Our work here is done."

Sheila's got the papers back in hand now, she's clutching them. "Nice to meet you," she says to Fitz. "Enjoy your day."

26

Back in the elevator with his father and a couple of other well-dressed business types—a man and a woman, each with leather bags, facing the same direction, watching the numbers above the door—Fitz feels different. Despite his jeans and sweatshirt, he feels professional, important even. He must be breathing in some secondhand confidence. His father looks pretty pleased. He's not literally whistling, but he may as well be: he has that kind of self-satisfied air. Fitz can hardly blame him. It's good to be him. A guy with his name on the door and a personal assistant. A guy who can sign his name and make something happen. It occurs to Fitz that this place is his father's stage, it's where he performs. He must feel like himself here, only bigger maybe.

They step out of the elevator into the lobby. "So what was that about?" Fitz asks. "Back in the office. The thing you signed."

"You really wanna know?"

"Yeah," Fitz says. "I wanna know."

"A motion," his father says. "That's what I had to sign. A motion to compel interrogatories."

"What does that do?"

"It's part of the discovery process," his father says. "Before we go to trial, there are some things we need to know."

That phrase, *discovery process*—it registers with Fitz. He likes the sound of it. "Questions you want answered."

"Exactly."

"So this stuff that your guy—"

His father corrects him. "Our client."

"Stuff your client needs to know. Stuff you need to know because, like you said, you have to tell his story."

"That's right."

"And the other guys, what do you call them?" They push through the revolving doors, his father in the lead, so Fitz has to wait to hear his response.

"Plaintiffs."

"Plaintiffs. They gotta tell you, right? They gotta answer your questions. You're *compelling* them."

"The judge will—we hope—but sure, that's how it works."

"Under oath?"

"Yep. Sworn statements."

"Because your client needs to know the truth. Has a right to know, isn't that so?"

They're on the sidewalk now, headed for the ramp. Maybe his father is surprised by Fitz's sudden interest in the workings of the justice system, by his passion for his case. But that's not it. That's not where he's going with this.

Fitz wants his own discovery process. He has some questions

he wants answered. When they're back in the car, his father's jacket hung up, Fitz's backpack positioned on his lap, seat belts buckled, that's when Fitz says what's on his mind.

"You're all mine now, right?" he says. "That's what you said. If I did what you wanted. If I did you that big favor. Which I did."

"Okay," his father says. He says it slowly, the drawn-out anticipation of something crazy.

"I just want you to answer some more questions," Fitz says. "That's all. I wanna do the interrogatory thing. With you."

Fitz has enough questions to fill up one of those long legal sheets. He could go and on.

"Questions," his father says. "Like?"

"Like, what happened? With you and Mom? With you and me."

Out of nowhere, Fitz feels himself choke up. He doesn't think his father notices, but it's those words, simple as that, *you and me*. The two of them stuck together like that. He turns away, looks out the window. He can't cave now. He didn't come all this way to go soft and blubber.

He can find his edge. He touches his backpack on his lap, feels the hard outline of the gun. He can compel. He remembers when he got in the car that morning, all snarly and full of attitude, his father thinking he was getting jacked.

"Come on," Fitz says. "One day you're thinking there's no one like her, and next thing, you're mailing it in from St. Louis. What's up with that? Something happened. Tell me what happened. That's all I'm asking."

His father's hand is on the shift but he hasn't put the car in gear.

"I wanna hear it," Fitz says. "The whole truth and nothing but the truth."

"All right," his father says. "You wanna hear about that? Fine. I can tell you that story."

27

"You were a good baby, a beautiful baby," that's how he starts. That's his once-upon-a-time. He says that Fitz was healthy, bright-eyed, curious. He had amazing blue eyes. It's just that he didn't sleep, at least not for long stretches. Two hours max, that's how long he'd stay down, often less than that, and then he'd be wide awake, demanding attention. Sometimes he'd be down for just a few minutes, then go off like a fire alarm, crying so hard that his face, even his head, turned red. Singing, rocking, jostling, walking—nothing seemed to help.

Annie was beyond exhausted, his father tells Fitz. "She was sleep-deprived. People say the words, but the real thing, it's hard to comprehend. How bad it is."

"Like torture," Fitz says.

"Exactly," his father says.

She wasn't getting a lot of help either. Her brother came over when he could. He had a good heart and a talent for goofy faces, but he was a teenager, his real world was somewhere else— the next date-dance, homework, hockey practice. One of her girlfriends from the diner used to stop by. But just like Dunc, she had a life outside of Annie's apartment.

"Annie never asked her dad to help, and he never offered," his father says.

Fitz could believe it. His grandpa was old-school. He couldn't imagine that he'd do diapers. You weren't going to catch him warming a bottle. From listening to his mom and uncle talk, Fitz could tell that his parenting style, if that's what you'd call it, wasn't suited for babies. He had the no-nonsense manner of an Army sergeant, which is what he'd been. They used to hold out their plates and he'd scoop food onto them. He called washing dishes KP. He wrote their names on cups and on every article of their clothing. Fitz knew that wouldn't work with a baby. Babies didn't care about keeping everything shipshape; they didn't come with a field manual; they showed no respect for standard operating procedure.

"What about you?" Fitz asks. "Were you still going out?"

"There's no going out with a baby," his father tells him. He says that he would stop by every couple of days, usually in the early evening before heading off to the library to study. He was trying his best to keep his head above water academically. He had finals and then, after that, the bar exam. He was sending out résumés. Still, he wanted to do the right thing.

But the baby scared him a little. He was so small, so delicate—so alien somehow. He'd hold him, but as often as not, as soon as he picked him up, the baby's lips would quiver and he'd start to cry. He was nervous and self-conscious, Annie watching his every move.

"I felt so awkward," his father says. "Totally inept. I had no real experience with babies."

Fitz imagines he'd never been really bad at anything before. He probably never received a failing grade in his life. *Welcome to the human race*—that's something his mom likes to say.

"I'd fumble with something, forget to support the head, and then Annie would step in. 'Here,' she'd say, 'let me take him,' and I'd hand you off.

"Back at school, in my study carrel," his father says, "things made sense. There were precedents, rules of evidence. There was a sense of order." He didn't love it, but he could do it. He could read through a case and identify the issues. More and more, he liked to argue, he enjoyed the back and forth, the give and take. Because he'd confided the fact of his fatherhood to only a single classmate, his study partner, Rory, he was able to keep it walled off, hidden away in a kind of bottom drawer of his life. In the middle of his familiar school routine, he could almost forget about it.

Fitz is trying his best to lean into his father's story, to meet him halfway. The bottom drawer—maybe that's where he's been keeping his dad these last few weeks.

"Kind of like a double life?" Fitz asks. "Like being undercover?"

"Yeah," his father says. "Something like that."

In Annie's apartment, his father says, nothing made sense. For one thing, Fitz had somehow mixed up days and nights. At three in the morning, the lights would be blazing, there'd be music playing, and he would be wide awake, wanting to play. In the middle of the day, the place would be dark, the blinds drawn,

Annie sleeping in a chair, the baby on her chest. The sink was full of dishes. She ate mostly peanut butter sandwiches, one slice of bread, folded over, food you make with one hand and eat standing up.

"I tried, I really tried," his father says. "I brought over Chinese takeout and some chocolates and once, a couple of books about babies. Dr. Spock, stuff like that. How-to books. I figured they might contain some helpful hints, maybe some advice about the night-and-day business.

"But Annie looked at me as if I were out of my mind. 'You think I have time to read?' she asked. 'Do I look like someone with time for leisure reading?' She didn't. Honestly, she looked a little crazed. More than a little crazed. Her hair was wild, and there were circles under her eyes. Makeup was a thing of the past. Mostly she wore the same plaid nightgown and a pair of woolly socks. Day and night. I started to wonder, do I even know this person? Who is she?"

Fitz feels defensive of his mom. He's not sure he likes hearing her being talked about this way. "What about your parents?" Fitz asks. "Did they know?"

"I meant to tell them," his father says. "I really did. I called one Sunday with just that intention. Annie was big as a house, and I felt ready to share the news. We'd found a crib at an estate sale and set it up in Annie's apartment. I was feeling optimistic, exhilarated even. For the first time in my life, maybe, I was doing something daring.

"Still, I knew it wouldn't be easy to tell my parents something they didn't want to hear. So I prepared and rehearsed—same as I would for an oral argument. I made notes. But when my mother answered, when I heard her voice, all that went out the window. I got as far as saying that there was a girl—kicking myself for calling her that—and that we were getting serious.

"'How serious?' my mother asked. She didn't ask the girl's name.

"'Semi-serious,' I said. 'Just a little serious.'

"'What does she *do?*' my mother asked.

"What you did—your job, your income and status, your prospects—to my parents, that was who you *were*." He glances at Fitz. Maybe he's wondering if Fitz knows people like that. Maybe he wants Fitz to believe that he is not a person like that.

"What Annie did was make me happy," his father says. "I could have told her that. Instead, I lied. I said that she was a law student, too, third-year, and when I hung up, I felt sick."

So you chickened out, Fitz doesn't say. That was your dare-to-be-great moment, your chance to declare your independence. But you didn't do it. You took a pass.

"When I was offered the position in St. Louis," his father says, "I was thrilled. A clerkship with a federal district judge was something special. It was my dream job.

"But now we had to figure some things out—we couldn't go on like this. For months we'd been speaking only in the present. But now I had a job out of state. At first Annie said that she was happy for me. She didn't want to hold me back. She never demanded anything from me. But now things were going to change. We had to make some decisions.

"It all came to a head one Saturday night. I was leaving on

Monday for St. Louis. We'd been talking all day, going around and around. We'd been talking for days, really. You were in a little baby seat. It had a handle and a little canopy. I had brought a pizza over, and it sat on the coffee table in front of us, untouched, just looking nasty. It seemed like some kind of accusation, even—who thought this was a good idea?"

Fitz understands. What kind of person brings cheese-and-pepperoni to this?

"We got into it again, really arguing this time. It was confusing, all my coming and going, that's what she was saying. It was making things worse. It wasn't right."

His father says he was ready to respond. There were some points he wanted to make. He wanted to take exception to some of the things Annie had said. Maybe he got a little bit, well, lawyerly.

"Annie cut me off. 'Oh, come on,' she said. 'Cut the crap. You can't have it both ways.' She said something about stepping up, being a man."

Yes, Fitz thinks. Yes! It's about time. Step the hell up.

"I guess I raised my voice then," his father says. "I just wanted to defend myself. Annie was being unfair. I can't even remember what it was I said. I was upset. Doesn't matter. It was loud, it was angry. The pizza box got knocked on the floor. The baby was still in his seat, right there on the couch between us. He startled. He started crying."

"That was me," Fitz says. "The crying baby." He feels like he needs to remind his father. This story—it's not all about him.

"You," his father says. "You started crying."

And Fitz isn't stupid. The pizza box didn't knock itself on the floor. Who's he trying to kid?

"Annie snatched you up in a flash. Held you close and just like that, you stopped crying. But your face was still beet red. You gave me a look. As if to say, what are you doing here? As if to say, get lost. That's just what you seemed to be saying. You are not needed here. I belong to her, not you. You're the problem. You're unnecessary."

Of course, Fitz feels like saying. Who needs a father?

"Annie told me that it would be best if I would leave. Best for her. Best for you. Best for everyone."

"So that's when you walked out."

"Stepped back," his father says. "That's what I thought I was doing. Just for the moment, like a time-out. A cooling-off period."

"Stepped back?" Fitz says. Can he hear himself?

"Annie told me that it would be better for all of us," his father says.

"Better for you," Fitz says quietly.

"I know how it must sound," his father says. "But it was temporary, that's what I thought at the time. That's what I told myself."

The rest of the story is pretty much what Mr. Massey calls denouement, falling action. After Curtis left town, Annie moved back in with Grandpa John and Uncle Dunc. Fitz knows things had been testy at home during her teenage years—back then his mom had a wild side—which is one reason she moved out in the first place. But now, they must have come together, because that's what you do, that's how family works.

As soon as he got to St. Louis, his father sent a check.

"I had no intention of being a deadbeat," he says.

Annie mailed him back a polite thank-you note. After that, he sent money every month, an amount that struck him as generous and gradually increased over the years. More at Christmas and around his birthday and at the beginning of each school year.

"While you were gone," Fitz asks, "did you think about us? Did you think about me?"

"Of course," he says. "Of course I did." Those first years, he says, he was working long hours, twelve, fourteen, even sixteen hours a day, living like a monk in a tiny apartment, but still, he would remember that baby smell, the way the baby threw his arms over his head after a feeding, milk-drunk. He hoped he was sleeping better.

"I called a few times," he says. It was awkward. Formal and polite. Annie thanked him for the checks, and he told her she was welcome, it was nothing. He asked how the baby was doing, and she said fine. She said everything was fine, and it was better this way. He agreed, and she agreed with his agreement. It was easier to believe her. Easier just to write a check, to believe he was doing the right thing.

When he came back to town once, he stopped by the house. He brought some flowers and a teddy bear. Her father was home, and he did not invite him in. "He'd had a few drinks," his father said. "He said that Annie wasn't home. He said that I wasn't welcome there. Told me what I could do with the flowers. I chose not to get into it with him. I called and left messages, but Annie didn't call back."

One day followed the next. It's just the way it is. His clerkship ended, and he took a job with one of the largest firms in St. Louis.

"Weeks passed," he say. "Months, years. I made partner. I thought about reconnecting, getting acquainted. I thought about it a lot."

"But you didn't do it," Fitz says.

"No," his father says. "I didn't do it."

They're both silent for a moment. For now, Fitz can't think of anything else to say.

"Every day you don't do something," his father says, "it's easier not to do it the next."

28

"You have a kid there?" Fitz asks. They've been driving around more or less aimlessly while his father talks. They've been out as far as the airport and the megamall, and are in Highland Park now. Edgcumbe Road. They've just passed the golf course and the theater where Fitz and his mom sometimes go to see second-run movies.

Fitz is trying now to keep the story going, trying to keep poking and prodding, trying to keep the ball in the air. But he's running out of gas. His father's story is slowly working its way through his insides, making him feel something. It's like a spiked drink, he's afraid, it's starting to make him woozy. Or maybe it's more like he just swallowed some broken glass—any minute, his insides are gonna start bleeding. Later, there'll be time to sort it out. Like one of the poems they read in Mr. Massey's class, he can chop it up, weigh and measure every little bit, analyze and interpret it, but for now he just wants more: more details, more words, more anything. "You got a kid in St. Louis, too?"

"No," his father says. He looks surprised. "No kid in St. Louis. No kid anywhere else."

"And you've really never been married?"

"Never."

They're at a four-way stop, and he motions for a momish woman in a minivan to go first. He may be a terrible father, but he's a courteous driver—Fitz has to give him that much. Go figure.

"I think maybe some people are just not cut out for that," his father says.

"For what?"

"You know—for that life. I think I'm one of them. I guess I've learned that much about myself."

Fitz wonders if it can really be that simple. Some people have a marriage allergy? Maybe. What about his mom? She went out on dates, more it seemed when Fitz was little. He can remember her primping, he can remember shaking hands with a few guys, playing the little gentleman, being interested in their cars, them being nice and kindly in an exaggerated way, trying to show his mom what good guys they were. There was Philip, who lasted longer than any of the others, who became a kind of regular around the house with his pressed jeans and full packs of sugarless gum. He was a computer expert, with a monster laptop Fitz played games on. Fitz liked him, but he stopped coming around eventually—not so much a breakup as a fade-out. His mom seemed kind of relieved. Recently Fitz even had some hopes that his mom and Mr. Boudreau, his French teacher, might hit it off on parent-teacher night. But she's never seemed especially eager to hook up with someone. She sure isn't one of those desperate middle-aged singles. Maybe she's got the allergy, too? Fitz wonders if you can inherit something like that. He wonders if he is doomed to be a serial loner, too.

29

They're still driving, on Snelling again now, passing a string of funeral homes, where they were about ten minutes ago—it's like they're in a holding pattern, waiting for permission to land somewhere. Fitz has a kind of movie in his head taking shape from his father's story. The scene of his father walking out, leaving him and his mom behind—Fitz knows already it's the one that's going to stick with him, it's the one he's going to come back to and watch again and again. He can almost hear the door slam.

In a Hollywood movie, Curtis would leave, but it wouldn't end there. There'd be another act. Later, he'd come back, and there'd be a tearful reunion. They'd both realize how stupid they'd been. But in real life—his real life—it never happened. It's not like his father was Bogey in *Casablanca* either, saying goodbye for some honorable motive. It was selfish, he basically said so himself. As if copping to that wipes the slate clean. It reminds Fitz of some politician's feeble blanket apology: sorry if I offended anyone, now let's turn the page, let's put this behind us. Meanwhile, whoever it is he's cheated is like, wait a minute, not so fast.

What really bothers Fitz is how easily his father seemed to step aside. He and his mom exchanged words, okay, they got worked up and said some things, he can understand that. She tells him, get out and stay out, etc. He goes to St. Louis, cools off a little, and then comes around with what, some flowers? It seems so lame. Why didn't he put up more of a fight?

"So tell me again," Fitz says. "Why you didn't come around. Why you didn't, you know, like, visit."

"She didn't want me to," his father says. "She said it was best for you."

"And you believed her."

His father doesn't say anything. Maybe he can't think of a plausible evasion. Maybe for once he's at a loss for words. He puts on his blinker, checks his blind spot, and changes lanes.

"You didn't make much of an effort," Fitz says.

"That so?" his father says. His voice is almost too calm, a kind of warning, a snake's rattle, which Fitz ignores. He hates his father's composure, that layer of lawyer cool.

"Come on," Fitz says. "Tell the truth. You didn't even try. You were so over us. Why don't you just admit it?"

"Look, my friend," his father says. Anybody who calls you "my friend" is not your friend—Fitz knows that much.

"Maybe you should have a talk with your mother," his father says. "Ask her who told me to stay away. Who told me that again and again and again. Who didn't return my calls. Whose father threatened me. Who refused me, who wouldn't let me in. Maybe you should take out your little piece and ask her some questions."

Fitz is startled by his father's tone, by his—what's the word for

124

it?—his *vehemence*. He did it fifteen years ago, and now he's done it again. This is the guy in the story. He's looking at him right now. Fitz can totally see it. The man can be nice when he's in control. In his office, surrounded by his people, he's Mr. Magnanimous. But push him a little, get up in his grill, he's a different person altogether.

Fitz flips up his hood. He's got nothing more to say. He's out of questions. He can't even remember why it seemed so important to get his father to talk, to tell him a story. A story! A bunch of words. That's all it is. It doesn't do anything. What's the point? Whatever his father tells him, that's not going to change anything. Those years, growing up without a dad, feeling jealous and unlovable and odd. *It is what it is.* Fitz usually hates people who say that. It seems so mindless, so all-purpose: you can say it about anything. But now it makes some kind of sense to him.

He looks out the window of the car and studies the nice houses they're passing. Brick and stone, some with winding driveways, all with beautiful green lawns and neatly trimmed bushes. Probably this is the kind of neighborhood where his father grew up. A suburb of Chicago—that's what he said. Maybe he was spoiled. Maybe he was one of those kids who never owned up, who broke something and just asked his parents for a new one, who messed up and walked away.

Fitz needs some music. Not his own—right now he's tired of his own sound, and he's not sure his father even deserves to hear any more from him and Caleb. He flips through the sleeve of discs and pulls out the Beatles' *Revolver*. He knows the album so well that when one track ends, he somehow feels the beginning of the next one even before it starts to play: "Eleanor Rigby" after "Taxman," "Good Day Sunshine" after "She Said She Said," the album unfolding song by song as inevitably as the alphabet. "Yellow Submarine" is one of the first songs Uncle Dunc taught him to play on the guitar—G, C, D, and A minor—and he can still remember the pride and pleasure he felt strumming while his mom and his uncle sang along. In seventh grade, when his Beatles obsession was in full force, Fitz wore a Sgt. Pepper T-shirt just about every day, and his mom even baked a birthday cake for George on February twenty-fifth.

Fitz is listening to George's famous backward guitar solo on "I'm Only Sleeping" when suddenly the volume cuts out. He looks over at his father and sees him holding down a button on the steering wheel—he's got built-in controls.

"I'm sorry," his father says. He says it softly, but even hooded, Fitz hears him perfectly. "I didn't mean to be short with you."

Fitz doesn't respond. All he can think is what a strange expression: *short with you.* "It was wrong to speak to you that way. I was wrong. I guess you hit a little close to home. I'm sorry."

Fitz imagines that it can't be very easy for his father to admit he's wrong. To apologize to a kid. *I'm sorry*—that can't be something he says very often. "It's okay," Fitz tells him. "Don't worry about it." Why not? Apology accepted. Forgiveness is free. And it's not as if he's been a model of good manners himself. Really, he's in no position to judge.

Whenever he's inclined to judge someone, his mom will usually call him out. She'll stick up for any underdog, criminals even. You don't know what they've been through, she'll say, you don't know what they've suffered, you have no idea what you would do if you were in their position.

If he were in his father's shoes fifteen years ago, what would Fitz have done? He's heard crying babies before, and they jangle his nerves. An angry woman showing him the door, giving him permission to leave, telling him, ordering him, really, to walk. Maybe he'd ease out the door, too.

One of Caleb's favorite all-purpose phrases is *can't imagine*. He says it when someone tells him about something foreign to him, outside his somewhat limited range of experience. Somebody's girlfriend woes, maybe, some kind of love triangle situation, say. Caleb takes it all in—he's a great listener—but that's about all he says. *Can't imagine*. It might seem unsympathetic. Most people want you to say just the opposite, that you get it, you understand—you can relate. But Fitz has come to appreciate his friend's honesty. He likes that he doesn't pretend to understand what he really knows nothing about. So what was it like to be his father back then? Fitz can't imagine. He really can't.

Fitz likes to think that he himself would have acted honorably. Manned up. Not taken the easy way out. He'd like to think that. But really, he doesn't know. He does know that he's taken the easy way himself plenty of times. It's easy to be brave in theory.

Fitz comes out of his hood and looks around. They're passing a school now. There's a line of buses idling outside. A woman in a reflective vest and a handheld stop sign makes them wait while a woman with a stroller crosses in front of them. School is about to let out.

It feels like the longest day of his life. It also feels like the shortest. They crammed a lot into a few hours together. They made some memories. You can say that much.

Here's the problem. As good as this day has been, it's been forced. Not freely given. They've fed sea lions, he's had a second piece of pie, he's heard about the exploding television, he's made his dad laugh. He's visited a law office and shared one of his songs. He's heard his father apologize. But it doesn't count, not really. What you get at gunpoint, that's not love. That's something else altogether. You can take a guy's car, but you can't jack someone's heart. It doesn't work that way.

Fitz can remember when he realized that Bethany, the teenage girl who lived across the street, was getting paid to play with him when his mom was out. He thought she liked playing with him, building with Lego toys, coloring, lying on the floor with all the figures from his *Star Wars* bucket around, arranging battle scenes. Then he saw money change hands, the smile on Bethany's face. To her it was a job. When he figured that out, he felt stupid and ashamed.

They have no future. This is a one-off. Fitz and his father, they're going to be known as one-hit wonders. Tomorrow, probably, he's going to get a restraining order, and it will be illegal for Fitz to go within a hundred yards of him. It was fun while it lasted.

Fitz thinks of those Make-A-Wish stories he sees on television from time to time. Some doomed, bald little kid spending the day with his sports hero, playing catch, getting autographs, going home with a big pile of gear. It's supposed to be heartwarming. But what about the next day? Fitz always wonders about that. And the day after that? It just makes Fitz sad.

"So now what?" his father says. They're stopped at the light on West Seventh. Fort Snelling is one way, downtown the other, the river is in front of them. "Where to?"

For a moment Fitz thinks his father is giving him a song. He tries—he likes songs with questions in them. "Now what?" That could be the title of something. He could see his father's questions becoming the chorus in some sort of existential anthem. But his heart's not in it. It seems like a lot of work. And for what? Scribble some words in a notebook—what would be the point of that? "Take me home," Fitz says.

RAINING TEARDROPS

30

Back on the west side, Fitz feels more like himself. On Summit Avenue, or in a downtown office building surrounded by suits and briefcases, he's an outsider, an alien, a spy. Here, he's just Fitz, a kid in his neighborhood.

They pass the gas station where he fills the tires of his bike, the pizza place where he and Caleb get slices and Dr Pepper with free refills, the hardware store where his mom gets little screws and such for her projects and is always smothered with attention by the old-guy clerks.

A few blocks away is the playground and park where Uncle Dunc used to push him on the swings, where he and his mom would spread a blanket and watch the Fourth of July fireworks from Harriet Island, where he still goes sledding with his friends in winter. Also, where he bought his gun.

Fitz looks at his father. Does it look like a slum to him? Compared to what he's used to, maybe it does. Does he see only chipped paint and crabgrass? Does it make him fear for his hubcaps and want to lock his doors?

Fitz doesn't care. He wouldn't mind if his father felt a little bit guilty: look at this miserable life I've inflicted on my poor son! He would like his father to think that he's grown up as a tough guy on the mean streets of West St. Paul, but it's not like that, not at all.

"Here," Fitz says when they come to his street, but he already has his turn signal on. On this block, Fitz knows the names of every family, present and past, he knows the names of their dogs, living and dead, he knows who gives out amazing treats on Halloween (Julia, the elderly piano teacher on the corner), who gives out sketchy-looking off-brand candy (the couple that listens to opera really loud on Saturday afternoons), who sits in the dark and pretends not to be home (Mr. Muscarella).

What does his father do on Halloween? Fitz wonders. There's no way any kids get into that building of his to trick-or-treat. For years he's probably been living in the same kind of place, some compound full of starched professionals, people just like himself. Does he even know what he's missing? He probably sits inside drinking fancy French wine and trading stocks online or something. Fitz almost feels sorry for him. Now Fitz hands out candy on Halloween: he and his mom pretend not to recognize Evelyn and Vivian, the little princesses from next door; she takes pictures, and Fitz gives them huge handfuls of fun-size candy bars, the good ones, Snickers and Milky Way. Fitz has learned that being with kids on Halloween is just about as good as being a kid on Halloween. What has his father learned?

31

Now Fitz feels like he is stalking himself. They're parked across the street from his own house. Fitz can see his bedroom window on the second floor. There's an empty can of Dr Pepper on the sill.

Fitz half expects to see himself coming up the walk from his bus stop, backpack slung over his shoulder. It's just about that time. He'd take the mail from the box, fish inside his pocket for his house key, and push open the door. He'd text his mom, tell her he's home. And she'd send back one of her perfectly punctuated messages telling him what he already knows: that there's food in the fridge, that he ought to get started on his homework, that she loves him.

They sit there, Fitz and his father, looking at the house. His mom spent the weekend working on her flower boxes and hanging baskets, white and red and purple. He doesn't know the names of the flowers, but they look good. Their house has a kind of old-fashioned vibe he likes—the flowers, a flag and wind chimes, the open porch, the wrought-iron rail, the gray clapboard and green shutters.

Fitz feels as if he ought to say something, but he's not sure what. He feels a stupid urge to apologize, for what exactly, he doesn't know. He knows that he says "sorry" a lot. Caleb called him out on it once after he excused himself for bumping into a chair—"Dude, relax," he said. "It's *inanimate*, it's not offended."

"You get paid by the hour?" Fitz says.

"My firm does," his father says. "Our clients pay for the time we work on their case."

"Plenty, right? They pay a lot."

"It's not cheap."

"So, like an hour with you, if I was your client, would cost me what, a hundred bucks?"

"More than that, actually."

"Two hundred, three hundred?"

"Something like that."

"So I'm costing you big-time. Wasting your time. I'm money down the drain."

His father starts to say something but then just raises his hand, palm out, fingers extended, like a stop sign, maybe, or a blessing.

At some point, Fitz needs to get out of the car. He needs to do what one of Caleb's favorite classic blues tunes says: *step it up and go*. Then it will be over. Their not-so-excellent adventure. Soon, but not yet.

He knows there's nothing he can say or do at this point that's going to make any kind of difference. Earlier in the day, he had some clear goals. Revenge—that was part of the plan, to make his father suffer for being a jerk. Payback, too, that was a piece of it, getting some of the time and attention he'd missed out on over the years. He wanted some information, too, he wanted to fill in some blanks. It's three o'clock now. Fitz is pretty sure that he's scared his father, at least a little, and he's heard some stories, and they've spent the day together. So what? Tomorrow he's gonna be his same old drifting self, asking Google what's the matter with him.

If Fitz is going to resume his regular life, he needs to get out of the car, go into the house, and text his mom. He should figure out the homework that's due tomorrow and get to work. Maybe he needs to lose his angst and stop whining and become an achiever. He should, unasked, do some household chore—start dinner, say, something to surprise his mom.

Still, there's a part of Fitz that doesn't want this to end. When he was a little kid, he never wanted to go to bed on his birthday. It was something special and rare, and he wanted to make it last. The day after his birthday, just another ordinary day, with no balloons and no cake—it always seemed a little sad to him.

"Okay," Fitz says.

"Okay," his father says.

Fitz isn't sure how he feels about him. Maybe he really does feel a little sorry for him. He's got a nice car, sure, and he's a legal-eagle big shot, but there's something sort of deficient about him, something lacking, something hollow. Fitz wouldn't trade places with him. But he doesn't think he really hates him. There's certain things about him that he could see himself liking if he got to know him properly. Fitz liked him feeding sea lions, he liked him at the diner, he liked him eating pie. At the office, not so much. It all depends. Fitz knows that he has not been all that likeable today himself, waving his piece and talking tough. Under different circumstances, it would be different. Under different circumstances, Fitz can be likeable, he can be fun to be around. He wishes his father knew that. He wishes he'd made a better impression today.

"Okay," Fitz says again. It feels like the awkward pause at the end of a class—anyone have any questions? As a matter of fact, Fitz does.

"Why Fitzgerald?"

"What do you mean?"

"I mean, why not Steinbeck? Why not Melville?"

"I was an English major," he says. "I read *Gatsby* in a course on the twentieth-century American novel. I loved it. I kept re-reading it. I'm not sure why. It just spoke to me somehow. The language. *So we beat on, boats against the current, borne back ceaselessly* . . . all that. It made me want to be a writer, too. It made me want to write the great American novel." He smiles a little, as if he's half embarrassed by the memory of his younger self, his susceptibility to beautiful language, his big foolish dreams.

"So it was you?" Fitz says. He was the Fitzgerald fan? "I thought Mom was the one who loved his stuff. I thought Mom named me."

"Oh, I gave her some books," he says. "I'm not sure she actually read them, though. I don't blame her. It was a little obnoxious. She thought I was trying to remake her, as if she weren't educated enough for me. But that wasn't it. I was just sharing my enthusiasm. But it came off wrong."

Fitz looks at his father. At one time, this guy dreamed about being a writer. He cared about words. Maybe he scribbled in a notebook, too. There's more to him than Fitz suspected. If they sit here long enough, there's no telling what he may discover about him.

"I'm pretty sure she read those books," Fitz says.

32

There's someone coming down the street. Even before Fitz sees his face, he recognizes Caleb's familiar walk. It's a slow shuffle, slower than you'd expect a young person to walk, as if he isn't really all that keen to reach his destination.

He's got his guitar in one hand, his amp in the other. There seems to be something coiled around his neck, nooselike. It could be some insane kind of goth choker, but that isn't Caleb's style. It could be a bike lock, but Caleb doesn't ride a bike (too dangerous).

"That's my friend," Fitz says.

Fitz lowers his window and leans out. "Hey, Caleb!" he shouts. "Caleb!"

Caleb just keeps walking, same glacial pace. It's impossible that he hasn't heard—they're no more than twenty feet away from each other. But Caleb doesn't even turn his head. "Caleb!" Fitz yells again, even louder this time. Still no response.

"I'll be right back," Fitz says to his father. He opens the car door and puts one foot on the curb. He pauses. He looks at his father.

The key's in the ignition. The motor's idling. What if he drives off? Fitz has already as good as said goodbye, handed back his father's phone and wallet, but still, the prospect of his taking off, of watching his taillights disappear at the end of the block, it fills Fitz's stomach with something like panic.

"I'm not going anywhere," his father says.

"Okay," Fitz says. "It'll only be a minute." He crosses the street and intercepts Caleb.

Caleb is still moving forward. He looks like someone moving across thin ice, that cautious. What he has around his neck, Fitz sees, is a super-duper guitar cable, something he's been talking about getting for weeks.

"Caleb!" Fitz shouts. He is maybe three feet away from him.

Now, finally, Caleb stops and turns slowly toward Fitz.

"What is up with you? I was calling your name. Didn't you know it was me?"

"I knew it was you."

"Why didn't you say anything?"

"I thought maybe you were trying to *lure* me somewhere."

"Why would I want to lure you anywhere?"

"You tell me. You're the predator."

"Cut it out."

"Who's the guy in the car?"

"That's my dad."

"Dude, you don't have a dad. That's like one of your trademarks. It's one of the things that makes you *interesting*."

"Everybody's got a dad."

"You know what I mean."

Caleb sets the amp down and turns toward the car in a way he must imagine is casual. It's not. "He's wearing a tie."

"I know," Fitz says. "He's my father, and he's wearing a tie."

"That's a really nice car," Caleb says. "Are you sure he's not an A&R guy? That's what he looks like."

"I'm sure he's not an A&R guy. He's a lawyer."

"Because we are nowhere near ready to sign with a label."

"Be serious."

"I've been trying to get ahold of you all day," Caleb says. "I sent you about a thousand texts. You've gone dark, dude."

"So here I am," Fitz says. "In the flesh. We can communicate in real time. What's up? You got the Monster—very cool."

"This is way beyond gear, Fitz."

"Okay," Fitz says. "What? What's worth a thousand texts?"

"Nora," Caleb says.

Nora? The sound of her name perks Fitz up a little. "What about her?"

"She's coming over."

"Nora Flynn?" Fitz says. "Here? When? When is she coming over?"

"Right here, right now," Caleb says. "Any minute." He smiles, a little wickedly.

"Get out."

"I saw her at lunch and asked her if she listened to the CD. 'Yeah,' she said. 'Loved it.' "

"She loved it."

"She loved it. You should have heard her, going on and on about Ruth Brown. She was obsessed. So I'm like, 'You wanna sing with us?' 'Sure,' she said. 'Absolutely.' 'Like when?' I said. 'Like how about this afternoon?' she said."

"I don't know about this," Fitz says. "I'm not sure if this is such a good idea."

"Since when are you anti-Nora?" Caleb asks. "Since when are you not her biggest fan?"

Fitz is trying to find some words to explain what's going on with him, how he's spent his day, why this may not be the best time to audition a singer, when he notices Caleb suddenly stiffen.

33

Fitz's father is standing there, smiling pleasantly. He's taken off his tie and rolled up the sleeves of his white shirt. If you didn't know any better, you'd think he was All-American Dad, home from work early.

"Hello?" Caleb says.

"Hello," he says, and extends his hand.

Caleb gives Fitz a quick glance and then takes it. He gives it a shake. "I'm Caleb," he says. "Pleased to meet you . . . Mr. Fitz's dad."

"Call me Curtis."

"Okay," Caleb says, but he doesn't.

"You're in the band," Fitz's father says.

"Well, yes," Caleb says. "Actually, right now Fitz and I *are* the band."

"I like your sound," Fitz's father says, and Caleb gives Fitz a triumphant look, as if to say, told you so, and Fitz suspects that now he will never be able to convince him that his father is not really a record executive.

"We need a drummer," Caleb says. "But it's not easy to find one."

"Drummers are famously problematic, aren't they?"

Caleb gives Fitz another look. *What planet is this guy from?* "Oh yes," he says. "Famously."

In fact, drummers have been, what he said, problematic. Fitz wonders how his father knows. He can't imagine that he's ever been in a band. In the past year they've played with only two human drummers: one was a kid with a fancy kit but absolutely no sense of rhythm, the other a kid they recruited from jazz band, who was always so busy with extracurricular activities and lessons—student council, Model UN, you name it—he was never available to hang out, much less practice.

"This is a big day for the band," Caleb says. "Today we're going to audition a vocalist. And I am pretty sure she's going to take us to the next level."

"Really," Fitz's father says. "That's exciting."

"I don't know about this," Fitz says. "I don't think this is such a good time."

"What do you mean?" Caleb says.

"I mean," Fitz says, "there's a lot going on. Couldn't we do this some other day?"

"Let me give you a hand," Fitz's father says, and picks up Caleb's amp. Caleb can be touchy about people handling his stuff, but this he doesn't seem to mind. "Thank you," he says, and leads the way, guitar in hand, up the walk to the front porch.

They've played out here before, Fitz and Caleb, sitting in a couple of lawn chairs. Maybe if Fitz's basement weren't a dank dungeon, they'd rehearse down there. Maybe not—Caleb loves playing outside. He thinks fresh air is good for musical instruments. And he doesn't mind a little ambient noise mixing with the music—likes it, really. If there were a train rumbling by, he'd be ecstatic. That would be pure Clarksdale. But even the ordinary clatter and hum of Fitz's neighborhood, he welcomes it into the sonic stew—a car horn, the sound of an airplane overhead, the *click-clack* of somebody trimming a hedge.

The problem with jamming out here is the electronics—how to plug in. There's no outlets on the porch. When Fitz's mom hangs Christmas lights, she does it with a complicated jerry-rigged network of extension cords that doesn't strike Fitz as entirely safe. Not that he'd ever tell her that.

Caleb tried once to run his amp's power cord into the house through the mailbox slot, but then was stuck in the corner of the porch, away from the chairs. Which is the point of Caleb's new heavy-duty, extra-long cord.

Caleb looks up at Fitz. "Don't just stand there, dude," he says. "Go inside and plug me in. And bring out your acoustic."

34

Fitz turns the key and pushes the front door open. Nothing has moved since this morning, of course, nothing has changed, but things feel different somehow.

It feels like a snapshot of a life—his life—that has been interrupted. On a bench in the front hall, there is a stack of his textbooks and notebooks, a folder containing the geometry proofs he dutifully completed last night, his thoughtful-sounding responses to Mr. Massey's questions about a poem by John Donne. Fitz was planning to skip, but he did his homework anyway. What did that say about him? It's hard now to imagine himself taking such pains again, working his way through another problem set tonight, adding and subtracting angles, trying to describe the speaker's tone, all that work, for what? Points?

He does a quick walk-through of the downstairs. In the kitchen, Fitz feels the weird vibe of Pompeii, the Roman city they studied in Global, buried by a volcanic eruption so quickly that everything was perfectly preserved, daily life flash-frozen, an archaeologist's dream come true. There is his cereal bowl and spoon in the sink. A jar of peanut butter on the counter where his mom made her morning toast, a knife balanced across the top. On the table is the multivitamin she laid out for him and he forgot to take. It looks sort of forlorn and sad sitting there, a little still life reminding him how much his mom loves him and what a rotten person he is.

There's one message on the answering machine, just as Fitz expected, received a little after nine o'clock that morning, about the time he was introducing himself to his father. It's from the attendance office at school, reporting Fitzgerald's absence, with a reminder that he'll need a note of excuse when he returns. Fitz has been planning all along to forge a note. He doesn't have the skills or guts to pull off a fake phone call. But he has discovered that with very little practice, he can reproduce his mom's signature reasonably well. She hardly signs her name the same way twice, but there's always a big Eiffel Tower A and an equally tall double-peaked M—the rest is squiggles.

Fitz deletes the message. For the first time today, maybe, he really feels that he's being dishonest with his mom. He doesn't feel good about lying to her. He's done just what Dominic and the rest of the detention crowd do every day—pull the wool over their parents' eyes. Turns out, he's pretty good at it, being sneaky. It's not that hard to do, Fitz is learning—except for the queasy feel of betrayal in his stomach.

Just then there's a noise from near the front door—a click and a soft scraping. Fitz turns, startled and frightened, his hands rising slowly, a man apprehended in the act. But it's not his mom, not the attendance police, it's just Caleb's cord snaking its way from the mail slot across the tile floor of the entryway. It seems alive, curious. He walks over to it slowly, grabs it by the pronged head, and plugs it in. He remembers what he came for and heads up the stairs and into his bedroom.

The guitar is poking out from under his bed, half-buried in dirty clothes. It supposedly belongs to Uncle Dunc, who bought it a year ago and conveniently left it in Fitz's custody. It's a dark mahogany, and he loves everything about it, even the smell. He strums a G chord. It has such a rich and beautiful tone, Fitz sometimes feels unworthy of it.

Before he heads back out, he takes a look at himself in the bathroom mirror. His hair may not look frightened, but it doesn't look good either. He scratches at it a little, moves it around his forehead. It doesn't seem to make much difference one way or the other. He holds his guitar up and makes an album-cover face, his best approximation of the Beatles' stare on *Rubber Soul*. He wants to look profound, he wants to look deep, but really he just looks worried—he looks constipated. He wonders whatever led him to hope that Nora might find this kid attractive, that his father might find him interesting.

35

When Fitz comes out of the house, guitar in hand, Caleb is sitting in one of the lawn chairs, playing scales, his father standing back a little, leaning on the porch railing, arms crossed, looking on approvingly. So often Caleb looks awkward and out of place, hunched and squinting, always at the edge of something, the perpetual square peg, but when he's cradling his guitar like this, bent over it, coaxing something out of it, speaking some special language to it, like a mother to her baby almost, he seems perfectly at ease, when he is most himself.

That's when Fitz notices her. It's as if his stomach knows who it is before his brain does: it does one of those little elevator drops. She is walking a black cruiser bike up the sidewalk, wearing jeans and a plaid shirt, a cascade of beautiful red hair spilling out from beneath her helmet. Nora Flynn!

She drops her bike, unbuckles her helmet, and comes up the porch steps, just as casually as if she did this every day. "Hey, guys," she says generally, taking in Caleb, Fitz, and his father, too.

Caleb, never really famous for his social skills, looks up and makes some rudimentary introductions. It's Fitz's house, but he's grateful that Caleb is willing to play the role of official greeter. He's not sure he could trust himself to do it right.

"Hey, Nora," Caleb says. "This is Fitz's dad." He motions with his head, his hands still on the guitar, playing something weird way up the neck, some unworldly chords, like the sound track for the slightly bizarre indie film they're all starring in right now.

"Hi, Mr. McGrath," she says, which is not his name, though there's no way she would know that. "I'm Nora." Her face is flushed from the effort of riding her bike, Fitz sees, and there are tiny beads of sweat on her upper lip. On a man it would be disreputable, but on her, it's adorable.

Fitz's dad is unfazed. He steps forward, smiles, and gives her hand a respectful shake. He doesn't correct her. "Nice to meet you," he says, and goes back to his perch on the edge of the porch.

To her he must seem like some garden-variety dad, home early from work or maybe taking the day off. He looks the part. For a guy with zero experience, he's not bad. He can pull it off.

"Hey, Fitz," she says, and he hears some sound come out of his mouth.

36

"So you dig Ruth Brown?" Caleb asks Nora.

"I dig every inch of her sound," she says. "Big-time. I've listened to that song about a million times. That girl can sing. I love her voice! She is so, what? Feisty? Is that the right word? Sassy? That tune has been in my head all day."

Nora scat-sings the first line of the song "Teardrops from My Eyes": "Dee de dee de dee, de dee de dee." She's blown in like some sort of meteorological event, a high-energy front Fitz can feel on his skin, transforming the weather on the porch from drab and testy to fun with a chance of joyous.

"I'm getting obsessed," Nora says. "Can you tell?"

Caleb smiles proudly. He's all about obsession. He gives Fitz a kind of one-of-us nod of approval. "Miss Rhythm," Caleb says. "That's what they called her. The girl with a tear in her voice."

"But there's no way you guys can play that song, is there?" she asks. Fitz wonders the same thing. There are horns playing on that recording, a whole big band backing her up. How in the world are the two of them—two kids on a porch with just a couple of guitars—going to reproduce that?

Caleb says, "We have our own way of playing a song like that, don't we, Fitz?"

Fitz nods and says, "Sure," noncommittal. He has absolutely no idea how they might play a song like that.

"Okay," Caleb says. "Take a seat." Fitz settles into the lawn chair next to Caleb, acoustic on his lap, and Nora pulls over the small bench. It's something Fitz's mom garbage-snatched last summer and painted a dramatic green. It's where she puts her book and tea when she reads out here. The three of them make a tight little grouping. There's no campfire, but it's got that feel. Fitz's father, meanwhile, is leaning on the porch rail. He's present, but distant, too. He's managed to make himself, if not invisible exactly, then at least inconspicuous. Caleb and Nora don't seem to think it's odd or creepy that he's here. They're not paying any attention to him, so neither does Fitz. If his father walked away, Fitz doesn't know what he'd do. But right now he looks fixed, he looks planted—doesn't look like he's going anywhere.

"Standard jump blues," Caleb says. "I've got some ideas. We do it in E, okay with you?" he says to Nora, and she nods.

Caleb noodles around a little on his guitar, adjusts something on his amp. He tunes his high-E string, then tunes it again. He fusses with his pickguard. By now, Fitz is used to his tics and rituals. He thinks he understands what this is all about—it's connected to his sense of awe for the music, his sense of his own unworthiness. Before the altar of the blues, in the shadow of Muddy and Wolf, Lightnin' and Sonny Boy and Little Walter and all the others, he gets the yips. He fiddles around some more, and finally, just about when Fitz is afraid that Nora is going to start to wonder what's wrong with him, he strikes a chord.

Before long Caleb is bouncing back and forth between E and A, getting a catchy little rhythm going, and Fitz can hear it, the verse of the song. It's happy and quick, which is surprising because the words are all about heartbreak and tears.

Nora is leaning forward, into the song, her head tilted a little. Caleb says the lyrics, feeding them to her in a kind of dull monotone. Nora repeats them, her lips moving, forming the words of the song, singing them, but so quietly Fitz can just barely hear her:

> *Every time it rains, I think of you*
> *And that's the time I feel so blue.*

They play it together a few times, Nora's singing gradually getting stronger and more confident, Caleb adding a little embellishment to his turnaround. It's some new riff, Fitz can tell from the look on Caleb's face, something he must have been working on. They sound good. Fitz admires the way they've hit it off, just how good their chemistry is, and he feels left out, too. It's like Caleb has whisked her away on the dance floor and left him on the sidelines, back at the punch bowl.

"Okay, dude," Caleb says then. "Give me something like the horn part on the record. See if you can mimic that."

Fitz remembers the song, those horns, a little bit, but he's not like Caleb, he doesn't have a freakish memory for tunes. He's too embarrassed to ask for help, though, not here, in front of Nora and his father, so he goes searching for those notes.

He quietly tries out a couple of combinations, but they're not only not right, they're not even close. It's like he's playing the bass part for some other song, in some other key, on some other planet. He tries something lower, something higher. Fitz feels as if he's blindfolded, lurching around a strange room, searching for something small and precious—he keeps banging and crashing into things. He's lost. Hopeless. It would be funny if it weren't happening to him. Nora glances in his direction, and now his father seems to be watching him with special attention. He feels himself starting to sweat. Bass Line Fail, he thinks. Epic Bass Line Fail.

And just then, almost as if he can feel Fitz's desperation, Caleb comes to the rescue. He sings the part, just two notes, the bass notes he wants Fitz to find. He keeps singing them softly, and it's all Fitz needs. He takes a deep breath. I can do this, he tells himself. I can totally do this. He goes up the neck and finds the first note right away. And after just a little bit of hunt-and-peck, he's got the other. Caleb gives him a nod. Fitz gets the tempo, and just like that, he's on board. He's in the pocket.

They play it through a few times, and just about when Fitz starts to forget the strangeness of the situation and finds himself feeling drawn into the music, Caleb raises his hand and calls a halt. He wants them to tackle the next part of the song.

"The chorus is a little tricky," he says. He tries out some chords. He mutters a little—to himself, to the guitar, maybe to the song. It's what he does. Fitz is tempted to explain, but Nora doesn't look disturbed.

Finally, Caleb's got a progression he likes. He runs through it slowly, his torso half-twisted so Fitz can see what he's playing—A, B-flat, and E. Nothing too exotic. Maybe Caleb was right, maybe they do have a way to play a song like this.

After about their eighth or ninth time through the chorus, Nora gives a little smile. "That's it," Caleb says. "That's totally it."

You wouldn't think you could smile while you're singing, but Nora can—she is. Her mouth is busy forming the words, but her whole face is alive with pleasure. It's like she's standing back a little from her own voice, from the song, listening and enjoying herself, catching Fitz's eye, as if to say, *isn't it something?*

Her voice isn't exactly like Ruth Brown's on the recording— how could it be?—but it has a certain attitude, sass, maybe that's what it was, maybe something all her own. She has a little bit of a tear in her voice, too.

Just then a brown delivery truck rolls down the street, slows, and stops next door in front of the Wilkersons'. The deliveryman—brown shorts, black socks and shoes, curly hair and mustache—emerges with a package. Fitz recognizes him, their regular guy. Somehow Fitz knows his name: Clay. Maybe it's stitched onto his shirt.

Clay jogs a package up to the Wilkersons' porch, deposits it there, and heads back to the truck. But halfway down the walk, he stops and pivots and turns toward them, toward the porch, toward the song. It's maybe the only time in his life Fitz has ever seen this man standing still.

They're coming around to the chorus again, and this time, maybe because they have an audience, Nora seems to give it a little extra:

> *Every single cloud would disappear,*
> *I'd wear a smile if you were here.*
> *So, baby, won't you hurry, because I need you so*
> *And it's raining teardrops from my eyes.*

"I'm feeling it," Clay the UPS guy shouts at them. "I'm really feeling it." And then he dashes back to his truck, puts it in gear, and pulls away.

Fitz is feeling it, too. The *it*—he could never spell it out, he could just point in its general direction, but that's okay. That's what music is for—to say things you can't put into words. It's got to do with his father, of course, and everything that has happened today, and his understanding that it's almost over. But it's also got to do with the music, the pleasure he feels in playing it, the connection he feels to them.

It occurs to Fitz that if he somehow got stuck here, forever playing his simple little part, tapping his foot to Caleb's jazzy rhythm, listening to Nora sing, watching her, he wouldn't mind a bit. To be able to sit so close to her and not have to say anything—it's wonderful. To hear her sing, to see joy and humor in her eyes—it's so much more personal, more intimate, really, than some chatter between classes.

He loves the feeling of collaboration, of teamwork. Each of them is contributing something—he maybe least of all, his simple little two-note bass line, but still. They're making something, together. Even his father seems necessary somehow. He's their audience, a witness.

37

That's when his mom's little red car comes tearing around the corner. There's no siren, of course, no flashing lights, but the car itself seems to exude a kind of 911 urgency. She pulls up right behind Curtis's car across the street and doesn't seem to park the car so much as drop it there.

Fitz should have anticipated this. He should have seen it coming. Because he didn't respond to her texts, because she hasn't heard from him after school, she's assumed the worst—the house is on fire, he's been abducted, he's fallen and he can't get up. In fact, nothing terrible has ever happened to Fitz, he's never been lost, endangered, or damaged, he's suffered barely a scrape or a bruise, but still, his mom can imagine catastrophe all day long.

Nora stops singing in the middle of a line. Fitz drops out, too. Only Caleb keeps playing, but softly now, shifting into some other progression, something ghostly.

Fitz's mom moves slowly, cautiously, up the sidewalk, steps around the abandoned bike, taking it all in, this little after-school party on her porch. She's wearing her usual casual work getup—a white T-shirt, jean jacket, sunglasses perched on her head—but her body language is tense and wary, like a cop responding to a domestic.

Fitz tries to imagine the scene from her perspective, to see what she's seeing. There's Caleb, guitar in his lap, playing something quiet and slightly ominous now in a minor key. He's plugged in today, but other than that, there's nothing really remarkable here, nothing she hasn't seen many times before—Caleb picking on the porch. But there's the girl. She's new. A redhead with a helmet in hand, nervously twisting the chin strap, who must belong to the bike, smiling, a little apprehensively, even guiltily.

And there's the man. Leaning on the porch rail, well dressed but disheveled, expensive haircut ever so slightly askew, his nice slacks and shirt looking sort of smudged and wrinkled, as if he's slept in them, flecks of Como Park mud on his wing tips. The guy is loitering, looming, he is inexplicably *lurking* on her front porch in the company of her only son and his best friend and some unknown girl. Fitz can see her taking it all in—no beer bottles, no contraband, everybody fully clothed—performing a kind of instantaneous damage assessment. Still, it could be bad, some low-level immorality in progress, maybe, a very peculiar sort of hostage situation.

She comes up the steps.

"Hi," Nora says. Her tone says, *please don't kill me*. She may not know exactly what's going on, but she seems to understand immediately that Annie is the alpha female. Caleb doesn't say anything, but he nods. Or maybe just bobs his head to the music in a way that suggests a greeting. No matter what Annie decides is going on, Fitz is pretty sure she won't blame Caleb. He'll get immunity. He's one of her underdogs, like the kids she works with—in her eyes, Caleb can do no wrong.

Just a few minutes ago, there was something almost magical happening here. That's gone now. Vanished. Now the whole vibe is *busted*, it's *party over*. Annie fixes her glare on Fitz's father. He's clearly the ringleader, the most dangerous character, troublemaker-in-chief.

"Annie," he says.

"Yes?" she says. Her voice sounds skeptical, suspicious. It's the way she talks to telemarketers. Maybe she doesn't recognize him. Fitz sees her right hand closing over her car keys. Making a fist. If he were in real danger, she'd go, Fitz doesn't doubt it—five-five, 120 pounds soaking wet, but if her son were in trouble, she'd throw down, in a heartbeat.

"Mom," Fitz says. "It's Curtis."

"Curtis?" she says. First sort of globally puzzled, as in *what's a Curtis?* or *which Curtis?* Then, finally, like, *really, you, Curtis?* "Curtis?"

"I can explain," he says.

"He can explain," Fitz says.

Annie waits. "Please do," she says. "Explain." She crosses her arms then, really crosses her arms, which she never does, assumes the classic this-ought-to-be-good pose.

"Fitz and I," he says, and pauses. It's a good start, Fitz thinks, a solid subject for a sentence. He can't wait to hear the predicate.

"Fitz and I," his father says, "we ran into each other."

His mom turns and fixes Fitz with a look. It's knowing, and it's murderous. It's as if in that instant, she intuits, in her scary omniscient mom way, everything, understands everything—his whole constellation of lies and deceptions, the tangled web he wove. She may not know exactly how they ended up here, but she knows it was no happy accident, no chance meeting. Before she can object, though, Curtis keeps it coming.

"We got a quick bite to eat," his father tells her. "That's all. We had lunch. And then I dropped him off. They were getting ready to rehearse, and they were good enough to invite me to stay and listen to a tune."

Fitz is grateful that he's not mentioned the gun. His unregistered firearm, the possession of which could land his butt behind bars. It's sitting right now not more than three feet from him, tucked in the front pocket of his backpack. He's grateful that he's not ratting him out. That he seems to be on his side. He likes the sound of his dad pleading his case. He likes the reasonable, unflustered tone, the way that the insanity of the day is getting smoothed into the reassuring shape of his story. He almost believes it himself. The man is good, Fitz realizes, he's probably worth every bit of his three hundred bucks an hour. He'd like to hire him to explain things, to be his own spokesman and personal persuader. He could explain to Mr. Massey why his term paper was so short; he could make the case to his mom that it wasn't his fault he managed to pull no better than an eighty-one in French. He could maybe even persuade Nora that he isn't the loser child of lunatics and deserves a second chance, that he is still worth getting to know.

Caleb is still playing, nearly inaudibly, finger-picking now, something sort of lyrical, ethereal even. Believing probably that so long as he keeps making music, he's safe. If he's shrouded in a sonic cloud, he must believe he is invisible, and no one will get up in his grill—that would kill him. He avoids conflict, hates confrontation of any kind.

There's silence now on the porch. Curtis has rested his case.

"There are going to be consequences," Annie says at last. She claims not to believe in punishment. Instead, she's all about consequences. The distinction is lost on Fitz. Consequences are the terrible things that happen to you as a result of your poor decisions. How is that not punishment?

Nora puts on her helmet. She buckles it and adjusts the straps. She's getting ready to leave, but she doesn't leave. Maybe she can't think of how to excuse herself gracefully from a mad situation. She probably doesn't know what words to say in order to extricate herself. Or maybe she wants to stick around just a little longer to savor the drama, to see what weird thing is going to happen next. It's hard for Fitz to imagine that she'll ever be back, that after all this she'll want anything to do with him, but he doesn't have time to grieve that now.

"Actions have consequences," Annie says. No one responds. It's like she's trying to incite something, light a match, get something started, but no one goes for the bait.

"I should get going," his father says.

"Yes," his mom says. "I think you should. Get going. I think that would be best for everybody."

His mom's face has an edge, something he barely recognizes and doesn't like, a hardness. Fitz wonders what gives her the right to speak for him. Since when does she know what's best for everybody?

Fitz feels an urge to stick up for his father—to take her on. To stick up for himself.

"You don't understand," Fitz says. He hears something weak and whiny in his voice, a sense of powerless outrage. "We didn't do anything wrong."

"We can talk about it later," she says.

"We sounded great," he says. The four of them on the porch, connected by the music—she broke that up.

"I'm sure you did," she says.

"You have no idea," Fitz says.

"We'll talk later."

"You haven't got a clue."

"Later," she says, her voice like a slap, like a slamming door.

38

It's the back of his head that sets him off.

Before that, right up until the moment Fitz loses it, things are calm and civil, everyone's conduct completely orderly. Everything has been smoothed over, for the time being at least, his mom pacified, if not pleased, their argument delayed, deferred. Nora and Caleb are halfway down the block, heading home together, Nora pushing her bike, Caleb doing his slow death march with his amp in one hand, guitar in the other, cable back around his neck. The regular programming of their lives about to resume.

Fitz says goodbye to his father on the porch steps. No handshake, just the blandest, most neutral words of parting—"bye," "so long"—his mom behind him straightening the furniture on the porch but really eavesdropping, it is so obvious, she's pseudo-straightening, trying to figure out what's happened, where things stand with them. But his father's tone and manner betray nothing—no sorrow, no anger either, nothing at all. If he feels anything at all—about Fitz, about what's happened today—he's not showing it. His face is blank. It's as if to him Fitz is Chip from the diner, nothing more, just some random guy, nobody special, someone he small-talks, exchanges pleasantries with, and then moves past—bye.

Fitz turns and bends down and picks up his backpack. His face feels hot. When he looks up, he sees his father walking away, toward his car, out of his life. The back of his head. After all this, after all they've been through, he still seems composed and confident somehow, unruffled. His hair perfectly trimmed, his shoulders square, his posture perfect.

And that's when it hits Fitz. A wild surge of emotion—rage, despair, a livid desperation roaring in his ears, some tsunami unleashed in him now, at last. He feels like a crazy bomb, ready to explode.

It's happening again. Fifteen years later, but it's the same thing. His mom putting the run on Curtis—on his dad. Chasing him away. Showing him the door. Telling him he better leave. And him taking it, no pushback whatsoever, walking away. Him like, okay, so long, as if nothing ever happened. As if *he* never happened. Showing him the back of his head.

Fitz feels a boiling inside. Something hot and dangerous bubbling up, demanding release. He'd scream but he knows his lungs and vocal cords could never produce a sound loud and desperate enough. What he feels is beyond the human voice.

He unzips the front pocket of his backpack and takes hold of the .38. Wraps his fingers around the grip. Right now, it feels just right in his hand. It feels receptive, as if it understands him. Maybe happiness really is a warm gun. It can be his voice, it can speak for him.

Fitz sets down his backpack and steps off the porch. He slowly raises the gun. He half expects someone to scream, but no one is even watching him. He's invisible. He's a ghost.

The wind chimes are tinkling. His mom is on her toes, picking dead leaves out of one of her hanging baskets of flowers. She's not even looking at him. His father is just stepping into the street.

Fitz cocks the hammer, pauses, then squeezes off a single round, upward, into the upper boughs of the big maple at the curb. The gun cracks and kicks, but he holds on. There's a puff of smoke around his hand and the smell of the Fourth of July, gunpowder. A small splintered branch, a couple of twigs with leaves attached, comes floating down and lands on the lawn. Fitz thinks suddenly of the family of squirrels that lives in that tree, hopes they're okay—he never wanted to kill anything; he wanted to make a noise, that's all.

"Fitz!" Annie shouts. She sees him now. "Fitz! Fitz!" It's like she's singing her own song, a song about shock and horror, and the only words are his name. "Good God!" she says. "Have you lost your mind?"

"No," Fitz says.

"Listen—"

"No," Fitz says. "You listen. Listen to me."

He holds on to the gun. He's not ready to give it up, not yet. He can't bring himself to point it at his mom but holds it waist-high, pointing upward. With his left hand he makes a kind of stop sign, a don't-come-any-closer gesture.

He can see Nora and Caleb halfway down the block, turned

back toward the house, frozen. Curtis has stopped and turned toward Fitz.

"Slow down," Annie says. "Breathe." It's like she's trying to compose herself and him all at the same time. "Take it easy," she says. Her tone is becoming professionally calm now—every day at school she deals with meltdowns and tantrums, opposition and rage. She's a pro.

Fitz's chest feels like it's vibrating. He may be crying, he's not sure. He wants to say something, but words are slipping away from him. "You are so *wrong*," he says. That's the best he can do, as close as he can get. "You think you're so right, but you're wrong."

"All right," she says. "All right."

"It's not all right!" Fitz says.

"Okay," his mom says. "I hear you. Put the gun down and tell me all about it. Tell me what's wrong."

It's like she's committed to listening now, but it's phony, strategic listening—it's like she's stalling until the SWAT team arrives.

"Everything," Fitz says. "That's what's wrong. You did everything wrong."

"I'm sorry," his mom says. She's so quiet, so still—it's how you face off with a mad dog. He hates himself for scaring her, but he can't stop, he doesn't know how to stop.

"I know what happened," Fitz says. "You didn't want me to know, but I know. You drove him away. And now you're doing it again."

"Fitz." It's his father's voice. He's standing now not more than ten feet away from him. Fitz never saw him move, but here he is.

"And you," Fitz says. He raises the gun. He has no problem pointing it in his direction.

"Me," Curtis says. He says this with a kind of sad calm, like a confession. He looks older than he did this morning, grayer. Is that even possible? Fitz wonders. He's read about people whose hair goes white after some terrible fright. Is that what he's done to him?

"You're a loser," Fitz says. "That's what you are."

"I am," he says. Now, this time, he's not talking to the gun. He's looking right at Fitz.

"I mean it," Fitz says. "You lost out. Missed out. On so much. On me. On us."

"You're right," his father says. His voice catches a little. He's inside some emotion Fitz can't quite read. There's sweat on his forehead, he's pale. He doesn't seem scared so much as feverish— it's like he's coming down with something.

But Fitz likes the sound of his agreement. He likes being right. Maybe it's just words. But it's something.

"I lied," his father says. "About coming back to St. Paul."

"What?" Fitz says.

"It was because of you," he says. "To be closer to you."

Fitz is trying to take this in, to understand what he's hearing.

"You didn't call," Fitz says. "You didn't visit."

"I was scared."

For the second time today Fitz is holding his father at gunpoint. He doesn't want to shoot him. *What do you want?* That's what his father asked him that morning when he got in the car. He didn't really have an answer. Now he knows.

He is going to make him say what he wants to hear. He can do that much, take that much of what he's owed. He is almost beside himself now, his hands shaking, tears flying off his face. But he understands now at last what he wants.

"I want you to say it," he tells his father. "Say the words."

Fitz has not shot him, but his father still looks wounded. His face is white and wet, with sweat, with tears. Fitz thinks for a moment that he may be having a heart attack.

Fitz lowers the gun. He feels his own foolishness, the insanity of it all. His doomed mission. Trying to extract love at gunpoint. He extends his arm to his mom. "Here," he says. "I'm sorry. It's over."

She takes hold of the grip of the .38.

"I love you," his father says. "I do." He says it that way, like a vow. "I do love you."

He bends forward at the waist, hands on his knees, shoulders heaving. It's as if before Fitz's eyes his father is crumpling, as if he's collapsing somehow. Deflating. Something is draining out of him—not just his bluster, not just his posture, his cool and confidence, but something more, his whole Curtis.

What's left is frail and sweaty, what's left is a tearstained mess, what's left is human. What's left, Fitz could love.

EPILOGUE

Fitz is sitting on the porch of his house. It is Saturday afternoon; he's waiting for his dad to pick him up. He's got his earbuds in, and he's listening to a recording he and Caleb and Nora made. A song that's almost but not quite there, one of Fitz's new lyrics. "No Safety." The tone of the lyrics is vaguely menacing, edgy, dangerous even, but Nora's voice brings some sweetness to it, some sad, knowing quality. It's about getting someone in your sights, taking aim, getting ready to hurt them or love them, it's not clear, maybe both. Caleb thinks they're onto something. If Fitz could only work out a slightly less boring bass part, and if he and Caleb could get together on the ending, it might be all right.

Nora is a full member of the band now, and they've got a new name: Dr. Eckleburg's Spectacles. It's a little shout-out to *The Great Gatsby*. Caleb likes the weirdness of it. He also thinks they should stay a trio. They've played together a few more times and the chemistry has been good, they sound good. They've worked up about a half dozen tunes, everything from more Ruth Brown to a bluesy, soulful version of "Something." Fitz has some more new lyrics in his notebook he'll show Caleb when the time feels right. One in particular might cause Nora some embarrassment, so he's keeping it under wraps for now. Forget about finding a drummer. More trouble than they're worth—that's Caleb's position. "Famously problematic," he's said more than once. "Curtis was so right. He nailed it." Caleb talks about Fitz's father quite a bit now, which he doesn't mind, sort of likes, actually, although he hopes he's got it through Caleb's head that his father does not work for a record label.

What happened last month, Fitz's little spree—they don't talk about it, Fitz and Caleb, at least not directly. Working their way through some Johnny Cash covers a couple of days earlier, when Caleb got to the line in "Folsom Prison Blues" about shooting a man in Reno just to watch him die, he gave Fitz what he probably imagined was a significant look, some eyebrow italics. I didn't shoot a man, Fitz felt like saying. I shot a *tree*. But he just kept playing, trying somehow to assume the air of a man haunted by a dark and guilty past.

Fitz is wearing the same jeans he had on the day he kidnapped his dad, only today he's got nothing tucked in his waistband. It's way more comfortable. It's been a month since then, and a lot has happened.

His father has disposed of Fitz's gun, for one thing. There was a buyback program. He knew a guy. No questions asked. "I wiped your prints," he told Fitz, "just to be sure." Fitz couldn't tell if he was joking or not.

His mom was right—there were consequences—but not

necessarily the ones he was expecting. She hasn't grounded him or anything like that. She didn't lecture him. Instead, she seems intent on treating him in some new, perhaps more respectful and adult manner. She's helped to arrange these outings with Curtis but always checks things with Fitz, doesn't presume to know his mind, asks for him to sign off: Saturday work for you? She doesn't quiz him afterward, even though he knows she's curious.

Fitz is pretty sure she's trying to make amends. It's okay, he wants to tell her. That stuff I said, my rant, I was in some altered state. I didn't mean it.

For his part, Fitz has tried to be scrupulously honest with her. He suspects his lies probably wounded his mom as much as anything he did that day, and he wants to earn back her trust. They've had a long talk, several actually, and Fitz has explained in detail what happened that day, his whole scheme—his misguided, foolish, crazy scheme, the likes of which he made clear he'll never attempt again. He's kept her excruciatingly well informed as to his whereabouts, the times of his departures and returns. He's found things to do around the house without being asked. Last night he made dinner, just spaghetti and salad and garlic bread, which he semi-burned in the broiler, but she was super-appreciative. He wants her to know that if he gains a dad, she'll be no less his mom. But there's no way to say that to her face, which is why he made dinner.

Fitz is pleased that things between Annie and Curtis have been cordial. The night before, he heard her on the phone, and at first he assumed she was talking to her brother, Uncle Dunc—she had that smile in her voice. But it was him. Of course, he's entertained the fantasy of the two of them together, but he knows it's unlikely, Gatsby and Daisy living happily ever after. You can't repeat the past. That's like the theme of the book. Still. You can hope.

Today Fitz and his father are going to the guitar store. Curtis says he's wanted to play for years but needs help picking out an instrument. He wants to get an acoustic, nothing fancy, something to learn on, and has asked Fitz if he'd be willing to show him the basics. Fitz tries to imagine himself teaching his father to play. Sharing some of the simple songs Uncle Dunc taught him when he was learning. "This Land Is Your Land." "You Are My Sunshine." Fitz can remember how long it took him to master a simple C chord, how his fingers ached. It's not easy being bad at something, being a beginner, especially for a grown-up—Fitz gives his dad credit for being willing.

His dad pulls up, parks in front of the house, and gets out of the car. He's wearing jeans and a striped polo and some pretty unfashionable sandal-like footwear. He looks a little like a model in a Father's Day ad. He looks like someone dressed him for the first day of dad school. Fitz doesn't mind. He likes that he seems to be trying. If he's a little nerdy in his weekend wear, that's okay with Fitz. It's part of the whole dad package.

So what kind of dad is he? Fitz asks himself. He's still not sure. Maybe he needs to do more fieldwork, more observation. Time will tell. Or maybe it doesn't matter. Maybe it's a stupid question. What kind of dad is he? My dad. That's who he is. In the end, maybe that's all that matters.

He's standing there now, right in front of him, his mouth moving, talking to him.

Fitz takes out his earbuds. He stands up. He feels his mom behind him, inside the screen door, watching.

"Fitz!" his father says. He is smiling. "You ready?"

ACKNOWLEDGMENTS

For support during the writing of this book, I am grateful to Canisius College; I am likewise grateful to my wonderful colleagues and students for their encouragement and inspiration. For sharing their expertise, I am indebted to Dave Alexander, Bill Gartz, Jesse Mank, and Ron Ousky. Thanks to Lon Otto for being a great reader and a great friend, to Jay Mandel for being such a wise and faithful guide for many years, and to Erin Clarke for her patience, kindness, and quiet brilliance. I am grateful, finally, to my family, Mary, Sam, and Henry, for the love and laughter that sustain me every day.

ABOUT THE AUTHOR

MICK COCHRANE was born and raised in St. Paul, Minnesota, and remains a passionate fan of the Minnesota Twins. He is the author of two adult novels, *Flesh Wounds* and *Sport,* and a middle-grade novel, *The Girl Who Threw Butterflies,* which *USA Today* called "a lovely coming-of-age novel . . . seasoned with small doses of Zen, baseball lore and history."

Mick lives with his family in Buffalo, New York, where he is a professor of English and Lowery Writer-in-Residence at Canisius College. You can visit him online at mickcochrane.com.